"Teach me to love you," she whispered.

We were in bed, but not touching. I turned on my side, facing her, and put my hand on her breast. "I'm not so sure you're gay, Margaret." I spoke softly. I wasn't accusing, just explaining. "I think you just want to be fucked by a woman, I've thought that all along. You say the right things, but they don't ring true, like you memorized stuff from a book or something. That made me angry the other day, but now it only makes me sad. And that's a pity because I like you . . . a lot." I could feel her heart beating faster. "But I want to make love to you," I said. "I'm wet from thinking about it."

"If it's wet you want, feel me." She guided my hand. Her pubic hair was soft, her thighs firm. She was dripping with moisture. Her legs opened wider and my hand slid easily to the small, raised organ that throbbed under my touch. I felt her shudder. Her legs moved farther apart.

About the Author

Catherine Ennis lives with her lover of over nineteen years in a region close to New Orleans and Cajun country and is retired from what she calls "work."

Presently, in addition to running a small business and writing for her own satisfaction, she experiments with gourmet cooking. She has restored a 1930 Model "A" Ford coupe which she enters in local parades and shows.

This book (Ennis' fifth) is a result of some of her most enjoyable research, and was fun to write because she didn't have to.

UP, UP
AND
AWAY

by
Catherine Ennis

THE NAIAD PRESS, INC.
1994

Printed in the United States of America on acid-free paper
First Edition

Edited by Christine Cassidy
Cover design by Bonnie Liss (Phoenix Graphics)
Typeset by Sandi Stancil

Library of Congress Cataloging-in-Publication Data

Ennis, Catherine, 1937–
   Up, up and away / by Catherine Ennis.
      p.   cm.
   ISBN 1-56280-065-5
   1. Lesbians—Fiction.   I. Title.
PS3555.N6U6   1994
813'.54—dc20

94-15977
CIP

To my Eva, for all the years

BOOKS BY CATHERINE ENNIS

To the Lightning
South of the Line
Clearwater
Chautauqua
Up, Up and Away

CHAPTER 1

This wasn't the first time a prison door had shut behind me, but I still felt the walls begin to close in when the guard slammed the metal door, leaving me the only occupant of the tiny room. Had I been claustrophobic, I'd be clawing the window bars in another minute.

I pushed my rolling cart to the formica table which was bolted to the floor in the center of the room. I took my VCR from the cart, centered it on the chair at the other end of the long table, the chair with its back to the door. There wasn't much light coming through the single barred opening, but a little light was better than none, I thought, glancing at the flickering tubes overhead.

Working automatically, and humming what I remembered from last night's concert, I plugged both the XLR cable from the mixer and the mini cable to the VCR, then the audio and video from the VCR to the TV. Once the camera was connected to the VCR, the setup was ready. I glanced at my watch. Plenty of time.

Inserting a test tape into the VCR, I made a sound check of each of the three mikes I had set on the table: one in front of the chair at the other end of the table, and one for each of the agents who'd sit facing each other across the table. The tape and the mikes were clear, no interference from the overhead fluorescents. I rewound and removed the test tape, reinserted a 120-minute broadcast tape, and cut off power.

There would be three people at the deposition, I had been told, Angelo Rancatore and two federal lawyers. Angelo was to be granted immunity and a new life under government protection for imparting information that would guarantee our local crime boss, Vinnie Scalio, a lifetime, and then some, in the federal penitentiary.

Since Angelo's life was on the line, it was decided that his deposition would do as much harm to Scalio as would his physical presence. My small company, Legalvision, Inc., was chosen to take the deposition because of our reputation for integrity and a high degree of professionalism. Also, we had been around longer than most and knew every lawyer and judge in Orleans and the surrounding parishes. The fact that my father has been a St. Tammany judge for thirty years probably didn't hurt either.

Now that I was set up, there was nothing to do but wait. I sat down and began filling out the form which would accompany the video. *This is the deposition of Angelo Rancatore,* I wrote, *taken at the Orleans Parish House of Detention.* I left the date and time blank because there was no way of telling when we would actually start. Then I noted the case jurisdiction, the number, the division, and signed my name, Sarah Ruth Bodman, Certified Legal Video Specialist.

I figured I had at least twenty minutes before the federal people got here. When they arrived, they'd call for Angelo to be brought down. I wandered to the window and looked past the prison yard, over the high concrete wall, and across the wide double boulevard with its grassy neutral ground separating the prison from the city's newest park. In addition to the bars, the window opening was covered with metal hardware cloth.

Some teenagers, both boys and girls, were playing soccer, running energetically back and forth across the sparse grass of the park's playing field. They were watched by a straggling crowd of adults and children, some standing, some sitting on the ground, a few in aluminum lawn chairs. What a great place for some bleachers, I thought. When I did tether flights there the next morning, I'd mention bleachers to the dignitaries gathered for the dedication. A baseball diamond had been planned, but maybe a soccer field should take its place, this being the nineties, and soccer so popular now.

The door lock turned. A guard entered first, took a long moment to scrutinize me and the video setup, then held the door open for a young woman. Our eyes met for an instant, then she looked at my video equipment, and the wires which were draped from the table to the wall outlets. Apparently they didn't represent a threat because she nodded at the guard, gave him a half-smile, then turned her attention to me.

"I'm Ms. Paige," she said. "You're Sarah Bodman?"

I nodded, matching her half-smile with one of my own.

"May I see some identification, please." She wasn't asking a question. Her hand outstretched, she flashed the same half-smile she'd given the guard. "I know you were probably checked ten times to get this far, but I'd like to see something with a picture."

I blinked. Yes, I had passed through the regular checkpoints. With a shrug, I moved from the window and bent to retrieve my red carry-all from the shelf under the utility cart. Apparently this was life threatening, because the guard moved to stand at her side and Ms. Paige's hand dropped to her shoulder bag.

"Whoa," I said. "Whoa. I'm just getting my wallet."

I upended the bag and carefully selected my wallet from the pile of junk that had cascaded over the table, some of it, unfortunately, landing on the floor.

I pulled out my drivers license and held it up so both could see. "Take it," I said to her. "Let's make sure."

She did. She looked at the license photo, then looked at me and, unsmiling, handed it back.

"We're okay," she said to the guard. With a grunt, he left, closing the door with a thud of metal hitting metal, snapping the lock behind him.

I stared at Ms. Paige for a moment, carefully scooped things from the table back into the bag, then knelt to gather the rest of my possessions from the floor. She knelt, too.

"Here." She reached under a chair to retrieve a half roll of chocolate mints. "These probably belong to you."

"Don't you want to make sure they're not little grenades? Go ahead, check them out," I said, ignoring her outstretched hand.

"If I thought they were, I would." She was serious.

"They probably aren't." We rose at the same time. "At least I hope they aren't. I've been eating them."

I snapped the catch and shoved my bag back under the cart.

"Are you always this uptight?" I asked. "I thought for a minute you were going to reach for a gun. Were you really going to shoot me?"

"Maybe. Maybe not." Her smile was less than generous. "I don't think I'm uptight, Ms. Bodman, just reasonably cautious."

"I didn't think firearms were allowed in here."

"Am I carrying one?"

5

I couldn't answer that. I only know how it had looked to me. I noticed she didn't take off her shoulder bag, but kept it hanging at her side. Was she carrying her life savings, perhaps?

The lock clanked, the door opened, and a young man in a business suit walked in, followed by a faded-looking man in orange coveralls. The guard entered behind them.

"Wait outside, please," Ms. Paige said to the guard. "We'll call you if we need you."

He stiffened, then turned and clomped out of the room. To my way of thinking, he closed the door somewhat harder than necessary but the two lawyers apparently didn't notice. They were busy seating the prisoner at the end of the table, where I had indicated, and sorting legal-looking documents into neat piles. Most of the pages had photos attached, I noticed.

I moved to my end of the table, facing the prisoner, and put earphones over my head but didn't cover my ears. Ms. Paige turned to watch my movements. She raised her eyebrows at me, clearly a question.

"I'm wearing earphones so I can correct any extraneous sounds." I pointed at the overhead lights. "Those things hum, for example, and with my mixer I can turn any mike up or down. I control the audio, in other words, so your tape will be clear and there's no outside interference with the sound." Unless this was her first deposition, she already knew this. I raised my eyebrows back at her.

I don't mind explaining what it is that I do, but this woman was beginning to get to me. I know I looked strange wired into the equipment, but there has to be a human element if the tapes are to be accepted in court. Ms. Paige must know this, also. The machines run themselves, sure, but only under experienced direction. Apparently satisfied, she turned back to her papers.

"Let me know when you're ready to go," I said. After a few more moments of shuffling papers, the young man looked at me and nodded.

"Please be quiet while I get everything started." I flipped the right switches, saw that all the tiny red lights were glowing, then I said, "Will the attorneys please identify themselves for the record, and swear in the witness." They did so, and the deposition began.

While a deposition is in progress, I have a form to fill out. It's a log that records who speaks, the time, and the counter numbers from the tape. I'm so busy keeping the record that I'm not really concerned with what's being said, only that video and sound are synchronized and both are free from outside interference.

Ms. Paige and the young man, who had identified himself as Andrew Turner, took turns. As each went methodically through the small stack of documents on the table in front of them, they held certain pages so that the attached photograph was visible to Angelo Rancatore and then to the camera. The photographs, I learned, were of those people who had been disposed of on order from Vinnie Scalio, the reputed gangland boss whose overthrow, partially due to today's testimony, was imminent.

Years ago, in my sophomore year, I left college with my roommate and became a diving instructor in the Florida Keys. I had a lot of fun, made plenty of friends, and was totally broke before the year was out. Half of my friends were mooching a living from the other half so, not wanting to live that hand-to-mouth existence, I returned to Louisiana. On the advice of my father's secretary, and since I was already familiar with court-oriented legalities, I learned to use video and audio equipment, took the "hands-on" test and became certified as a videographer.

At the same time, Mabel, who had been my father's secretary for over twenty years, quit my father's office, became a court reporter, and now works with me. She has also been "aunt" to my brother and me since my mother's death a week after my birth. She was upset when her services weren't needed for this deposition.

"What do you mean they don't want a transcript to match your video? That sounds very strange to me. I don't know that it'll hold up in court."

"All I know is I'm getting paid to take a deposition, and they specifically didn't want a court reporter in on it." What else could I say?

When I learned the facts of the deposition from Judge Webster of the criminal court, it began to sound very strange to me, too. If a deposition was to be complete, it should be done in the time-honored way, with a transcript to accompany the video.

"Maybe," I said to Mabel, "they don't intend to use it in court. Could be they just want to make a movie."

Well, here I was, making their movie starring two lawyers and one very nervous criminal.

CHAPTER 2

My tape would run for an hour and twenty minutes, and it was edging up to that point now. If they didn't finish soon I'd have to use another tape. I took my eyes off the monitor, looked at the papers still on the table, and tried to guess how many pages were still to go. Ms. Paige — or could it be Mrs.? she wasn't wearing a ring — had been talking about banking, and Angelo Rancatore was vigorously shaking his head.

"I told you, I was a gofer in them days. I drove,

kept my mouth shut and my ears closed. Can't tell you anything about what they did with the money."

"But you were a collector, weren't you?"

"Yes, ma'am, later on I was. But I only went my route. I turned in whatever I was handed and didn't ask no questions."

"I find that hard to believe, Mr. Rancatore. Surely in twenty years you learned more than where the bodies were buried."

"I told you, there wasn't any bodies buried. We never did that. In Belle Chaise we'd cross over both levees and dump 'em in the river, at a deep place off the bank. A concrete block took 'em to the bottom, and the current took 'em down river from there."

"Well," said Andrew Turner, "that certainly explains why none of these people have surfaced, if you'll pardon the pun."

Paige raised her eyebrows. "Can we get back to the money question?" she asked, clearly exasperated.

Rancatore was shaking his head, looking harried, as if he had said the same thing a dozen times, which by my estimation he had.

"Don't you think I'd tell you if I knew? Sometimes I'd take packages to banks in another parish, but I don't even know that there was money. Only I couldn't think of anything else to be taking to a bank." He smiled at this flash of brilliance, showing a mouth full of large, white teeth.

"We've probably covered what we intended to cover, don't you think?" Andrew Turner looked anxiously at Ms. Paige. "Is there anything else?" He began picking up papers, stacking them in a neat pile.

"No," Ms. Paige said with a frown, "I guess that's

10

everything. We haven't learned anything new, that's for sure. As far as I'm concerned, it's been a waste."

"Well, I told you what I know. We been over it a hundred times already. You're still gonna protect me, ain't ya?" There was a whine in Rancatore's voice. He seemed to shrivel in his chair as I watched.

"Yes, of course we are. Arrangements have been made to take you from here tomorrow at noon. You'll be fully protected all the way, even after you assume your new identity." Andrew Turner gathered the rest of the documents from the table. Briskly he stacked the two piles together, then placed the pile in his leather briefcase. "I will accompany you tomorrow. It's part of my job."

Rancatore looked at Ms. Paige. "You comin' too?"

She shook her head. "No, this is it for me. I'll be leaving Monday, back to Boston."

"You have about a minute left on this tape." I interrupted. "If there's anything else to be said, say it now."

"I forgot we were still recording. I don't want that last part on the tape . . . about my taking Rancatore out of here." Turner was shaking his head. "Can you erase that?"

"No. Erasures or deletions invalidate the tape."

"So what do we do?" He was looking at Paige, who closed the catches on her briefcase and stood it upright on the table.

"By the time this is put to use Mr. Rancatore will be long gone. I can't see that we need to do anything." She pushed back her chair. "Tell the guard we're ready, please."

That was something that had bothered me all morning. My chair, at the opposite end of the table from Rancatore, faced the door. I was the only one who could see the door, unless Paige or Turner turned to look. Rancatore was sitting with his back to it. For all of the time we'd been in the room, the guard had his face almost pressed against the glass window. It was doubtful that any sound had carried, but he certainly would have gotten an earful. I figured he was supposed to keep his eyes on us, but it still made me uneasy.

This wasn't the first deposition I'd taken in the House of Detention. It was the first in this room, however. Other times, the guards had locked the door, and stood outside and out of sight. Besides, the doors were made of thick glass and metal.

I began unplugging and winding cords. Paige stood by the table, watching.

"Anything I can do to help?" she asked.

I didn't answer. Instead I held up the video. "Who gets the tape?" I asked her. "For security, I was told not to make a duplicate. I can hand everything to you right now." I leaned over and put the video on the table next to her purse, which she had placed next to her briefcase.

The guard was standing in the doorway, holding the door ajar, Rancatore and Turner waiting just behind him.

Paige looked at the guard briefly, then turned back to me.

"I'm not leaving yet., she said over her shoulder. "Close the door, please. I'll let you know when I'm ready."

How now, brown cow, I thought, what's this? I unplugged the final cord and began winding it.

"I'll do that." Paige took the cord from my hand. "Unless, of course, you don't think I'm capable."

Never one to beat around the bush, I said, "Lady, you sure change your spots in a hurry."

"These are the same spots, Ms. Bodman. The difference is that I'm not on duty. I'm on my own time now." She handed the cord back to me, neatly coiled. "What's next?"

"Well, ah, you can fit these covers, I guess. And while you're doing that, I'll finish this." I had already taken the tab off the tape, so it couldn't be recorded over, but I needed to finish the paperwork for my records. I wrote the time, initialed each page, signed the log, then put it into a brown folder next to the video.

I sat back to watch her trying to fit the right cover on the video machine. "Everything's numbered on the inside of the cover, and on the right side of the machine, so you can match whatever goes together," I said. "Did all that for a student once, made it faster and easier."

"Then I won't have to learn a thing, will I? Just know my numbers." She smiled, a real smile this time. There was a flicker of amusement in her blue eyes.

Very nice smile, slender figure, faint pink coloring on lips and nails, good legs, tiny waist, ample bosom, about my age, and with short, lustrous black hair curling around tiny ears. I hadn't been that close, but I'll bet her perfume was light and clean-smelling. Altogether to my taste. Definitely to my taste, except for her personality. I'm a bossy person, everyone says. She's a bossy person, I knew from brief experience. Could anything happen here? Why was she helping me get my stuff together?

"I thought if I gave you a hand, we could have coffee together, maybe a sandwich or something." She wasn't looking at me, her attention presumably on the recorder. "I'm in town only for the weekend, and I don't know a soul." She slipped a cloth cover over the monitor. "How about it? I'll treat."

"Sure," I said, "I've never turned down a free coffee or whatever. We'll go in my car, take the equipment home, then come back to the quarter and eat. How about some hot boudin?"

"I don't know what that is, but if it's edible, I'm for it."

She walked to the door. From the back, she was definitely to my taste.

Her pounding brought the guard. "Will you take this for us, please." Pointing to my rolling cart, and without a backward glance, she marched out of the room with me, my cart and the guard trailing along behind.

I live alone in an apartment just off of Esplanade Avenue, near the river. Except that there's never anyplace to park, I love the area. I have a large bedroom, a living and dining room, a small kitchen and a huge bath. My bedroom also has French doors which open onto a balcony overlooking a tiny patio. Privacy is assured by ancient banana trees which hug the corn cob fence separating the patio from the sidewalk.

I knew it was my lucky day when I pulled into a

space directly in front of the old mansion that housed my apartment. Together, Ms. Paige and I pushed the cart up the ramp from the street and into the wide hall.

"My apartment is the first door on the right. Please do come in," I offered graciously as I pulled and she pushed the cart through the doorway.

"Where's your office?" she asked. Simply standing in the center of the living room, she could see into every other room.

"I share space in an office building on Magazine Street. Most of my stuff is there. But we can leave all this here —" I pointed to the cart. "— because I have a deposition Monday afternoon, and I won't have to go over there after it."

She nodded. "Good thinking, Ms. Bodman."

"How about Sarah, that's my name. What's yours, Ms. Paige?"

"My name is Margaret. Margaret, not Maggie."

I was beginning to get vibes from Ms. Margaret Paige. They were faint but I am an expert at detecting invitations, no matter how tentative or disguised they may be.

To make things easier, I asked, "Do you want to go for coffee or shall I make some here?" I figured it would only take one cup to get her to the bedroom.

"Go, I think." She was sitting on my sofa, legs crossed, and the side slits of her skirt revealed many inches of thigh.

I let her see me looking there, then at her breasts, then into her eyes.

We held that gaze for a long moment, then she rose. Without a word, she walked to the door. Her hand on the knob, she turned to look at me.

"But, I am definitely interested," she said. This almost floored me. I determined to be my most charming while we ate, then I would translate 'interest' into an evening, maybe a whole night, of sex. She had definitely turned me on.

We walked to the Cafe du Monde, had café au lait and shared a plate of beignets. "Now, a couple of blocks up Bourbon Street and I'll introduce you to some good eating."

"What was that we just did?"

"That was to whet our appetite. Not," I added, "that I needed stimulation . . . if you know what I mean."

"Of course I know what you mean. You're not talking about food any more, you're talking about sex. Sex together, you and me, right?"

She certainly got to the point, no fooling around, no dancing around the bush. No foreplay either, maybe? I think her way of questioning was to raise her eyebrows. She raised them now. I waited for the question.

"Have you ever done it in your balloon? While it was in the air, I mean?" She could change directions in a hurry, too.

"How do you know about my balloon?" I didn't have to ask, "Done what?" I knew exactly what she meant.

"You were checked out three ways to Sunday. I know you're twenty-six, single, a balloon pilot, a videographer with your own business, a lesbian, not in a relationship at present, and that you've been known to sleep around. You did not graduate college, you rode a motorcycle for a while. Your mother died shortly after you were born, and you are very close with your father, who is a judge, and your brother, a Mississippi River pilot. You are —"

"Whoa." Frowning, I took hold of her arm. "I don't really like hearing all that. It pisses me off, if you want to know."

"That's something else I know about you. You have a quick temper, which I believe is directed at me right now." She flashed that little half-smile.

"Damn right," I said angrily. "But there's one thing maybe you *didn't* know . . . I don't take that kind of crap off of anybody!"

"No crap, Sarah. It's just what you do, who you are. We had to be sure that what took place with Rancatore today wouldn't go any further. Yours wasn't the only name on the list, but you were the one chosen."

I was still holding her arm. She moved so that my hand was touching her side. Her blue eyes looked directly into mine. "And I meant it when I said I was interested. More now than before, in fact. And after we eat boudin, maybe we'll head back to your apartment for something a little more exotic." Her arm squeezed my hand against her breast.

Not at all mollified, I stopped, pulled my hand away and turned to face her. "Lady, you are leading me on. I don't think you're really interested at all, just teasing because you know I'm a lesbian, and you're away from home, and who's to know if you fuck a woman. It might even be fun, right? And you certainly won't get pregnant." I was warming to the subject. "Honey, you've come on too hard and fast for me. I can tell fake when I hear it. Best thing for you is to get a cab from here, go to your hotel and find yourself a man."

On that bright note, I turned and walked back the way we'd come. I heard her call my name. My anger was still at the boiling stage, so I didn't even look back.

CHAPTER 3

"Mabel, she had me so mad I almost decked her, right there on Royal Street. What is it with straight women anyway?"

Mabel answered me seriously. "Honey, they probably find the thought of sleeping with a woman titillating. I think they think all lesbians want to get under their skirts. There's probably some kind of power thing, too."

"She acted like she had plenty of that. Some bossy bitch, I'll say that for her." I drained my glass of tea, shifted the receiver to my other ear and asked, "You're still going to help me tomorrow morning?"

"Of course I am, Sarah. I promised, didn't I?"

"Well, something could have come up. Anybody with eighteen nieces and nephews can't always anticipate a change in plans, you know." Talking with Mabel had a calming effect on me. I don't think I've ever in my whole life heard her raise her voice in anger. My father was incredulous when she left him to work with me, but Mabel told him that I needed her more than he did, what with starting a new business.

"My experience with you, Alonzo, will be invaluable to Sarah," she had told him. No one else in the world called my father by his first name. He was simply called "Judge" by everyone who knew him.

And I did need her. After Florida, my life was falling apart. My lover had sailed into the sunset with a wealthy yacht owner, a woman twice her age, and I was devastated. Somehow our love for each other had turned from something simple and beautiful into constant disagreements over every-thing — money, choice of friends, even when and how we'd make love.

Mabel had known I was a lesbian before I could spell the word. It was to Mabel that I went after my first sexual experience. I was just entering my teens, the girl was several years older, and why she wanted scrawny me is a mystery to this day. Not having a mother, I always went to Mabel with my fears and tears. I still go to Mabel with my problems. She has over fifty years of experience to call on when I need help. More important, she's the only person with whom I can talk openly about my sexual preferences.

"Don't worry, honey, I'll be there at seven tomorrow. You just have the coffee hot."

"Lonnie said he'd bring two friends, so I should have enough help to get Ragtime up. All you'll have to do is keep the kids in some kind of order. I wouldn't want to land on anybody's head."

As it turned out, landing on somebody's head was to be the least of my worries.

I was up a few minutes after five. I called the weather bureau's special number, reached my friend, Jerry, and got the scoop on the prevailing winds. When an ordinary person calls the bureau, they're given a report similar to what the weather people say on TV. But when pilots ask for a weather report, they want more. They need to know wind direction, patterns, altitude, speed, temperatures — any information available to make an informed decision about flying that day.

My balloon, Ragtime, was only going to do tether flights, but I needed to know that there weren't any sixty-mile gusts up there, waiting to slam me into the ground.

My brother, Lonnie, driving my truck which was garaged at his home in Metairie, was at the park at six. With its Tommy Gate, my truck holds the envelope, basket, burner, fan, and all of the other equipment needed to get Ragtime safely into the air, and keep her there until I decide to come down.

Lonnie and his two river pilot friends had already unloaded Ragtime, laid her out, and were positioning the fan for cold inflation. Lonnie started the fan's gasoline engine, and the whirling wooden blades began filling the balloon with air. Ragtime has seventy five thousand five hundred cubic feet of cloth, and cold inflation takes half an hour. While his friends filled her with air, Lonnie and I attached the basket and the burner and straightened the lines. I lit the pilot, and when she was nearly filled, rolling and beginning to billow at the sides, I got in the basket, opened the valve and ignited the burner. I gave her several long blasts. Slowly, as the roaring flame heated the air inside her, she lifted from the ground, setting the basket upright.

Almost seven o'clock. Craftspeople were setting up their displays in the spaces allotted to them, and cars were pulling in all over the place. There was a crowd around Ragtime, everyone looking up in awe as she swayed slightly in the soft breeze. Lonnie and his helpers had secured the three tethers that would hold her in place; one line was tied to the bumper of my VW, one to my truck, and one to Mabel's bumper.

I had decided to take six children up at a time. The basket is square so two can stand at a side, leaving one side for me. It was Mabel's job to see that no one carried anything into the basket. It's tempting to spit, or drop something, over the side. We have done tether flights before, and Mabel knows the score.

I spent the necessary five minutes going over my checklist. Lonnie and his friends held the basket steady on the ground.

"You're not going anyplace, Sarah, so why do you

22

have to check every tiny thing every time?" Lonnie was impatient. I knew he thought only a woman would check everything every time. A man, of course, wouldn't have to.

I was smiling as I checked off each item in turn, ignoring him. I knew of several male pilots who practically rebuilt their equipment each time they flew. I would never fault a pilot who cared about safety.

Lonnie has an older-brother complex. He's been up with me so many times he thinks he can fly without having to know all that "junk" pilots learn. He can get the balloon into the air, yes, but I'm the one with the license, and I wouldn't want to be a passenger if something happened.

Usually, I have three fuel tanks aboard. I had Lonnie take out two so there'd be more room. He put the full tanks in my truck, ready to be exchanged for an empty. I knew I'd empty all three before noon, when the heat outside the envelope would almost equal that inside.

Finally, I was finished checking. I pulled on my leather gloves and yelled to Mabel, "Let's fly!"

We'd brought a step stool for the little ones, and they clambered aboard. Then, while they squealed and screamed, I gave a long pull on the blast valve. It roars as the gas ignites, heats the air in the balloon, and causes us to rise gently from the ground.

Ragtime was the undisputed hit of the park's dedication. I must have lifted off a hundred times, but there was always a crowd. Many youngsters had been up more than once; I had begun to recognize faces.

A few hours later, I had used two tanks and was now working on the last one. I tapped the fuel gauge. About a quarter full. Enough for one more ascension.

There were two teenaged boys and three youngsters in this load. The older boys were fascinated, asking questions faster than I could answer. They were especially curious about the burner and its roaring flame. I explained about the pilot light, and that it was sort of like igniting a gas stove.

I gave each of the older boys a turn lighting it, but then the little ones wanted to do it, too. I had to refuse. They were too short to reach the handle, and it wasn't safe to lift them up.

We made a slow descent, touching down so gently that the boys said they didn't even feel the basket touch the ground. As I handed the little ones over the side to Lonnie and Mabel, I said loud enough for the crowd to hear, "Think that's the last ride, folks. I'm almost out of gas." There was a chorus of groans, but I shook my head. "No more today."

Mabel touched my arm. "I think there's someone here to see you, Sarah," she said. "I think it's your new friend."

"Oh?" I looked around. Margaret Paige was standing not ten feet away. I looked right into her eyes, then I deliberately turned to Mabel.

"Yeah, that's her. How did you know?"

"There's just something about her, and the fact she's been inching closer, watching you, for the last hour."

"Well, I don't care what she's doing." Lonnie was holding the basket steady, so I heaved myself to the edge, and swiveled my legs around so I could slide to the ground. "Well, she can watch all she wants. It doesn't cost anything."

Mabel put her hands on my knee, holding me in place. "Just a moment, young lady. Don't be rude." She was shaking her head and frowning, an expression I didn't often see.

I took a deep breath and turned a scowling face to Ms. Margaret Paige. She was smiling slightly, and I began to feel absolutely childish. I hopped to the ground, took a few steps toward her.

"You here to see me?" What a stupid thing to say! Of course she was here to see me. She was wearing a running outfit, loose beige pants, a long-sleeved matching jacket, cream-colored shirt with the collar out, running shoes. Everything expensive. Everything absolutely perfect.

"I came for a ride." She was standing motionless, an ivory statue with slightly windblown hair.

"Well, the rides are over." I said gruffly. I started to turn away but her hand caught my sleeve.

"You said you were out of gas...almost. So couldn't we just have a quickie?"

I caught my breath. A quickie was what I had wanted from her last night. A quickie to take the edge off, then slow, delicious sex the whole night through. Was she baiting me again?

"No," I mumbled. "It wouldn't be safe."

"Of course it would, Sarah. Why don't you take your friend up." A smiling Mabel faced us. She took Ms. Paige's elbow and urged her towards the basket.

I couldn't believe Mabel. "Are you serious?" I asked.

She nodded. "While you're up, I'll walk over to the drink stand and get us something cool. Now, you go ahead."

I jerked my head at the basket. "Well, come on, Ms. Paige, let's get it over with." Somehow I choked over calling her Margaret. It sounded too friendly. I looked up. Ragtime was beginning to sag but she still had plenty of air.

Lonnie had already put away the step stool and untied two of the tethers. Grinning, he helped lift Ms. Paige into the basket, but I heaved myself over the side.

Our lift off was perfect. I cleared my throat. I'd just pretend she was a tourist, I thought, someone I've never seen before. I felt strangely embarrassed at my own behavior and wanted to make it up to her without being too obvious.

"Ah, look over that way." I pointed. "That's the Superdome, that white mushroom-shaped roof."

She turned as I pointed, but turned towards me. "Did you get over what was bothering you?" she asked, moving closer.

I didn't intend to answer that. "And behind us," I said, as if she hadn't spoken, "look back there, that's where we were yesterday. See, that's the window of the room where —" My mouth fell open. I yanked her arm. "My God, look at that!"

Several men were exiting the back of the building. As they made their way down the steps, a black car with blackened windows swerved into the driveway, drew up in front of them and stopped. The car's four doors opened, a man came out of each door, and they all began shooting at the men on the steps.

26

None of this could be seen from ground level, but we were higher than the concrete block wall that hid the prison driveway and the first floor of the building.

"Oh, no! That's Rancatore and Andrew!" Paige leaned over the basket's edge. "They're being killed!"

"We're next," I screamed. One of the men had turned and was looking up. I saw the muzzle flash as he began shooting directly at us. "Let's get out of here!" I yelled. "Grab the valve, yank the valve . . . give it gas . . . pull the handle, Margaret!"

She stared at me for a second then seemed to realize what I was saying. I saw her arm reach in the right direction, but I had yanked my knife from the holster and was too busy hacking at the remaining tether to see if she knew what a valve was. I darted a glance at the ground, saw more flashes.

"Come on, Margaret!" I gritted through clenched teeth.

Either she knew, or else she guessed, which handle to pull. The gas caught with a roar, the sound like a freight train rolling over my head. The tether parted. We began to rise, not very fast for the first second or two, then we went up with a lurch.

I knew when the bullet hit her. I heard her grunt. I watched as she let go of the handle and clutched at her side with both hands. Unbelieving, I stared at her. She blinked several times and said in a very quiet voice, "Oh." Then I looked down at her jacket and saw blood oozing between her fingers, not a lot, but blood nonetheless.

I was aware of little crackling sounds, little pings.

I reached up for the gas valve and yanked. Standing there, rooted to the spot, with one arm in the air, I couldn't do a thing for her. But if I didn't get us higher than bullets could reach, we'd both be as good as dead.

CHAPTER 4

Ballooning is quiet. Except when igniting gas to heat the air inside the envelope, there's not much sound except, perhaps, for the creak of the basket as you or your passengers shift from one side to the other to get a better view of the ground. I listened, but couldn't hear any more of the little spitting sounds the bullets had made as they tore through the heavy wicker of our basket.

My hand clamped to the handle, we had moved up very high and drifted many blocks away from the park and the House of Detention. Already, we were over the outskirts of New Orleans, passing over the Bonnet Carre spillway and the raised highway that partly skirted Lake Ponchartrain. My burner flame sputtered and died. I let go of the valve. Whatever was happening on the ground was out of our control. We were drifting west towards the Manchac swamp, a destination certainly not of my selection,

I turned to Margaret. "Are you . . . ?" I swallowed. "What can I do?"

"I don't know," she said, eyes wide, her hands pressed against her side. "Shouldn't you be steering or something?"

This struck me as the funniest thing I'd ever heard. "I forgot to bring the steering wheel," I said. Levity was inappropriate here, but I was frightened. She could be dying.

She read my mind. "I don't think this is fatal, but I certainly would like to sit down. Help me?"

I put my arms around her and held on as she slid down the side of the basket, coming to rest on the floor with her legs outstretched, hands still covering her side.

There was more blood now. She lifted her eyebrows a fraction. "Hell of a mess, isn't it?"

"I think I ought to do something, but I don't know what, do you?" No sense acting like a know-it-all. More than basic first aid was called for here, I thought.

"Maybe we should look at whatever this is. But, Sarah, I'm afraid . . . what if all my insides fall out when I move my hands?" My startled glance told me she was kidding.

She could make light of it, but I couldn't. My

answer was serious. "I think there'd be more blood. Or something." There was no way I could joke about being shot.

"You do?" she asked. At first, she'd been white as a sheet, but there seemed to be more color in her face now. "Well, let's try, shall we?" She moved her hands a fraction but I stopped her with a touch to her shoulder.

"Wait, wait!" I said. "Maybe that's not such a good idea!" What if part of her did fall out? That was possible, wasn't it?

"Oh ye of little faith," she whispered shakily. Then she moved her hands. Both of us stared down at the bloody jacket.

"Have to unzip it, won't I?" She looked at me, her eyebrows raised in that way she has. I hadn't noticed how blue her eyes were. "Won't I?" she asked again.

A deep breath. "No, let me." As gently as I could, I pulled the zipper down all the way, exposing the silk shirt tucked into her waistband. It was bloody, of course. Inch by careful inch I pulled the shirttail out, then began unbuttoning from the bottom button.

"Here," she said. "Let's do it right." And she unbuttoned the blouse completely from the top down. "I don't want to look," she said, holding the blouse open, her gaze centered somewhere over my shoulder.

She wasn't wearing a bra. My eyes went first to her breasts, then to the blood oozing out of a small, dark red depression about two inches to the right, and three inches higher than her navel. Then I looked at a raggedy oozing place a few more inches to the right, and slightly higher.

31

"Margaret, looks to me like something went in here then came out there." I pointed. "I think you were sort of grazed. Kind of."

"You mean I haven't been dealt a mortal wound? It sure hurts like one." She looked down at her bleeding flesh, then looked up at me. Those blue eyes again, appealing.

Gulping, I said, "I usually have a first-aid kit with me, but I leave it in the truck when I do tether flights." Then I said in my most whining Southern accent, "Gee, Miss Margaret, I sure wish we'd brought the truck with us."

"I didn't know you were such a funny lady." She shifted, wincing slightly, then she gave me that little half smile, the one I remembered from prison. Her voice low, she said, "It hurts a lot, Sarah." Her blouse was open but I averted my eyes.

"Well, you've been shot . . . bound to hurt. But Margaret, with those bullets coming at us from underneath, think of how much worse it could have been. We could have been hit, both of us, in any number of awkward places. I know it's bad but I think you're luckier than you realize." I wasn't trying to make light of her being shot, but now that I'd seen she wasn't fatally wounded, I wasn't so shaky myself. At least, I thought, we were alive.

"You're trying to make me feel better, and I thank you for that, but should you let us drift like this. Shouldn't you land us someplace? I need to get in touch with my office." Her expression was anxious.

I hadn't looked over the side in many minutes. I didn't have to. I knew where we were.

Just to make sure, I rose to my feet and leaned over, looking in all directions. I was right, as usual. I know enough about our particular area of Louisiana to be able to place myself even without a map. We were beginning to drift lower, but I couldn't do anything about it. We were out of gas. My only option was in landing. I could land at whatever speed we were now falling, or I could yank the red cord, letting most of the air out of the envelope, and drop to the surface like lead.

I put my hand on her shoulder. "Margaret," I said, "I am the captain of a sinking ship. We don't have any gas, can't control our drift, can't do anything but land. That's to your liking, I know. What you won't like is where we have to land." I squeezed her shoulder, then I lifted her left hand away from her side and cradled it in mine, blood and all.

"Where?" she asked, squeezing my fingers.

"We will soon be slap dab in the middle of the Manchac Swamp, a place where neither of us wants to go. No sane person wants to be in this swamp. Except for an occasional poacher or escaped convict, that is." Did I have to tell her that? Why frighten her more than she was already?

"Can't we just drift over it? Go around it?" *Please,* her expression said, *tell me that's what we're going to do.*

"We don't have any choice, Margaret, ma'am. We'll be landing within the next half-hour or so, whether we want to or not. The swamp stretches for miles . . . and the wind will take us out over the Gulf of Mexico if we don't land in the swamp. Do you want to drown? I don't have life preservers, you know." Not much of a choice, but it was all we had.

"Please," she said, covering her side with both

hands again. "Please don't tease." Were those tears? Had I made her cry?

"I'm not teasing," I said gently. "I'm trying not to frighten you, honest, but we're in a hell of a fix. It won't last forever, though. They'll know where we've drifted. They're organizing a search party right now, I'll bet. We just have to be uncomfortable for a while, then they'll find us and take us home. You'll see."

I sat beside her, put an arm around her shoulders. "In a little while I'll be busy trying to put us down. I want you to get in the corner and squeeze yourself into as little a ball as you can. Bring your knees up and hug them to you. Keep your face snugged down. We'll land in trees, and it may get rocky for a while if we drag around, but chances are you'll be okay." I hugged her and lightly kissed her cheek. "I'll take care of you as best I can," I promised.

"Okay." She turned to me. "You'll let me know just before we hit, won't you?"

I nodded. We were almost nose to nose already, so I wasn't surprised when she leaned and lightly touched her lips to mine.

"That's what I wanted to do all yesterday," she said simply.

"Me too," I told her.

I was watching for a clear space but there wasn't one in sight. The ground was a carpet of green trees. We were already low enough that we raked some of

34

the taller ones. I knew Margaret could hear the limbs brushing underneath the basket. She didn't say anything, just remained huddled in the corner, her face hidden from me.

"Okay, Margaret, we're going down!" Just a breath away, the trees seemed to thin. As good a place as any, I thought. I tugged the vent line, felt Ragtime lurch slightly, then coast lower . . . and lower. The basket hit first, of course, twigs scraping and breaking as we raked over and through the trees. It was probably less than a minute, but it seemed to take an eternity before we jerked to a stop, impaled on a huge, broken branch.

Ragtime, still slightly airborne, passed over us. Caught by tree limbs, the basket stopped Ragtime's forward motion, and the envelope began to settle slowly. I swear I heard her sigh as all her beautiful rainbow colors came to their resting place on the treetops. I knew there would be little left of her to salvage from this place.

The basket was leaning at a slight angle, but almost upright. Margaret was still huddled in a ball, arms around her legs, head buried on her knees. When the basket stopped moving, she looked up.

"Is it over?"

"We're down. At least down as far as the treetops. I don't know how secure we are, so maybe we'd better try for the ground right away. Think you're able to do some climbing?"

"Maybe, maybe not," she said. "If I can't hold on at least I'll stop falling when I reach the ground, won't I?" She started to get up.

To help, I put my hands under her arms and lifted. Her groan was involuntary, but finally she was on her feet. I laced my fingers together to give her a foothold, and after a moment's hesitation, she let me heave her to the basket's edge. She perched precariously on the rim, one hand covering her side, the other with a death-grip on the gas tank valves. I could tell that she wasn't up to climbing down a tree.

"Stay on the edge, Margaret, and I'll help you swing your legs over the side." Now that she was ready to get off the basket, I had a flash of genius. "Let me go first, and you slide down between me and the trunk. Put your feet where mine are, and hold on to the tree. Lean back into me. That way, I can help steady you, I think. At least, I'll try."

That's the way we did it. I'd find secure footing, then Margaret would place her feet on mine and rest between me and the tree. I'd wrap my arms around both and we'd kind of slide to the next available limb. It took forever but I finally stepped on soggy ground. Margaret leaned against the tree, holding her side. Her face was pasty white again.

"You sit here," I told her. "I'm going up after some things."

"Do you have to? What things?"

"I want my knife, and there's a thermos of coffee behind the gas tank. Who knows what I may want?" I really wanted to gather all of Ragtime to me, to embrace all of her and somehow fly away to home and safety.

Somewhat distracted by the horde of mosquitoes that had instantly landed on every bit of exposed flesh, Margaret nodded.

"Don't forget to be home by supper," she said primly.

36

* * * * *

I made three trips before I had stripped the
basket of everything I thought I wanted to have with
me when we were flown out of here. I'd get another
balloon, of course, but I could use what I'd recovered:
a few personal items, the burner, the altimeter,
gauges from the tank, tools, my thick rubber floor
mat, and especially my maps. I made a neat pile
under the willow tree.

While Margaret gulped down a cup of cold coffee,
I fished out the fuzzy yellow pullover I had always
carried as a spare. "Put this on, you'll feel better in
something clean. I'm going to cut strips from your
shirt to wrap around you, so you won't have to hold
yourself, and so nothing spills out. That be okay?"

In answer, Margaret started unbuttoning again.
Good thing for the knife, or I would never have been
able to make strips from her shirt. She sat, naked
from the waist up, as I wrapped her as tight as she'd
let me. The blood had stopped oozing but started
again after I'd tied the final knot. Just a little,
though.

I hoped my smile was reassuring. I wanted to do
more for her, but didn't know what form "more"
should take. "There," I said, "feel better?"

"Not really, but you probably do."

"Well, I'm a doer. Always have to be busy. My
next assignment is to get us away from this tree.
There's too much mud underfoot so before we sink
out of sight, we're going to find someplace drier. You
may have to walk a ways. Think you can?"

"It's debatable, but I'll try."

With me half-carrying her, we sloshed through

37

water and mud until we found mostly dry ground under a clump of swamp willows.

"Will they be able to see us under here?"

"No, but I'll run out and wave your jacket when they get here. They'll find us."

We weren't settled before I heard the far away drone of a plane's engine. It didn't sound like a helicopter, which was the only way we could get out of here.

"They're probably just trying to locate us so the rescue copter won't waste time looking," I explained. When the sound was almost overhead, I picked up her blood-stained beige jacket. "Hang in there, Margaret, we're almost out of here." I started back the way we'd come.

The plane came nearer, its motor sounding louder. Then I heard another, even louder noise. I can recognize machine-gun fire. I've seen enough movies. There was a long burst over the envelope and basket, then the plane was past. It turned, came back, and bullets thoroughly raked the area again, I could hear leaves and limbs shredding. I had stopped in my tracks, looking up, seeing nothing but green, listening to the plane and the gunfire.

Margaret grabbed my shoulders from behind. Startled, I swirled and almost knocked her down. I held her, or she held me. Terrified, we clung to each other.

"What's happening, Sarah! That's gunfire!"

"And if we were under those trees, we'd be dead. Let's get going!"

We ran, sloshing through knee-deep water, staggering through palmetto clumps, climbing buried tree trunks, until Margaret stopped.

She was breathing great gulps of air. "I can't go any farther, they'll just have to shoot me."

"No," I said as I helped her ease to the ground. "They're gone. I don't hear them anymore."

When our breathing calmed, Margaret said, "Had to be Vinnie Scalio."

"It probably was, but why?"

"They saw you looking down at them while they shot Rancatore and Andrew. You can identify them. Why else would they try to kill you?"

"Well then they're after both of us, not just me. They were bound to have seen two heads peering over the basket."

Margaret nodded slowly.

"And they don't know if we're dead or not. Will they be back, do you think?" I asked this calmly, my tone as reasonable as I could make it.

"Of course they'll be back. Count on it."

CHAPTER 5

We sat against a tree, our bottoms resting in mud. Our shoes were soaked, our pants wet to the waist, and sweat dripped from every pore. I was still trying to put some sense to what was happening, to get a handle on whatever it was that was nagging at the back of my mind.

Finally it came to me. "Margaret, aren't you supposed to have a gun? I thought all FBI people carried one. You had one yesterday, didn't you?"

"I'm not with the FBI. Actually, I'm an assistant district attorney in Boston, and I've never owned a gun in my life."

Astonishment must have showed on my face. I felt my mouth drop open. "But they told me two federal agents were going to handle the deposition. Why would they tell me that if it wasn't so? I thought you and Andrew were agents. You sure acted like agents."

"It's a long story, but I suppose we have time." She drew in a deep breath. "From three Boston banks there was trail of money leading to New Orleans and Vinnie Scalio. Somehow, our office learned of Angelo Rancatore's defection, and we thought he could help us with details. I was part of the task force assigned to, ah, get the goods on Scalio and the others who were channeling money through a number of banks in several states."

She paused, brushed a mosquito from her cheek, took another breath. "We felt that someone from our office should actually talk with Rancatore, and I was the only one who could be spared. I am an agent of sorts, Sarah, just not with the FBI. You must have misunderstood."

Thinking back, I nodded. "I guess I did. Sometimes I don't listen as carefully as I should." Well, that settled that.

"Do you think we can drink that water?" She pointed to a puddle near our feet. "I'm really thirsty and that cold coffee didn't help much."

"I don't think I'd try it." Tadpoles were visibly frisking at the edges. "I'm going back for the stuff I salvaged from Ragtime. There's still some coffee in the thermos, it'll at least wet your mouth, if nothing else."

"Not without me, you don't." She started to get up.

"Hey, wait! I can get there faster without you. You rest here, and I'll be back in a jiffy, okay?"

She sank back against the tree, visibly relieved.

I got slightly lost a couple of times. The trees and the underbrush all looked alike. If we had left tracks in the mud, they'd settled back to whatever they looked like before we passed. I knew where west was because the sun was not quite directly overhead, and so I sloshed northwest, heading toward the place where I thought we'd landed. My biggest hope was that I could find Margaret again.

There was nothing I could use but my sense of direction, which was excellent when I had a compass. My hand compass, however, was in the stack of things I'd taken from the basket, that and the bug repellent which would be even more welcome than the compass.

About halfway to my cache, I heard what I thought was a chopper. Relieved that we were finally about to be rescued, I started running toward the sound. The ground underfoot was only a thin film of water over mud, but the mud was like glue. My left foot went up to the calf in a hole, and I left the shoe there when I pulled out my foot.

To keep balanced, I hopped on my right foot

while trying to dig for my shoe, the whine of the engine getting louder as I searched frantically in the muck. What the hell, I thought. I sat down firmly in the mud and plunged both hands in the hole. Mud up to my armpits, I rescued the shoe. I forced the soggy shoe back on my foot and pushed myself upright.

I stood still for a moment, to locate the motor's sound. It seemed farther away and, no, it was not the *whump whump* of a helicopter. The continuous hum was definitely that of a small, single-engine craft, and it was now coming closer. Unmoving, with both feet slowly sinking out of sight, I listened.

The plane was moving from west to east and, from the sound, would probably pass almost directly overhead. It did pass overhead, then turned and came back from the opposite direction, but a short distance or so farther to the south than the first pass.

They were executing a search pattern, with our highly visible multicolored envelope as a starting place. I recognized that. But what were they going to do when they located us? There was no way the plane could land, only by fishing us up and out with a chopper could we be safely hauled out of here. Maybe they were just trying to find us so they could radio our location to the chopper. Or, maybe they were just trying to locate us so they could shoot at us again.

With that in mind, I decided I had better get back to Margaret. By foot, and as fast as I could run through the swamp, she was at least twenty minutes from me. But she was only seconds away by plane, so it would certainly get to her before I could. She would flap her arms, jump, yell, and try to get their attention, of course. I wanted to get to her, to warn her not to do that, but there wasn't time.

I also wanted the thermos, the hand compass and my knife. Since I couldn't reach her before the plane did, I forged ahead in what I hoped was the direction of my stash.

I was running frantically from tree to tree, searching the ground, when I saw, standing out like a beacon against all the green, the cream-colored scraps of Margaret's blouse where I had dropped them earlier. Almost sobbing with relief, I rummaged through the pile, grabbed the thermos, the knife and my pocket compass, and headed back at a furious trot, splashing water and mud in all directions.

The plane passed over once more, but I squatted under a bushy clump so I couldn't be seen. When the drone of the engine faded, I jumped to my feet.

"Margaret," I hollered. "Margaret!" I found it very difficult to run at my fastest, leap over logs, detour around trees and yell her name at the top of my lungs at the same time. Out of breath, I paused to rest for a second. "Margaret." I sobbed. "Where the hell are you?"

Margaret touched my shoulder. Startled, I twisted.

"Easy, there," Margaret said, catching my hand with both of hers. "It's only me."

"Oh God, I thought something had me."

"No, but if we don't get out of this clearing, something will have us, and soon. Hear the plane?"

"I think that's the same one. They'll shoot if they see us."

"Let's move over to those trees. They're thick enough to hide us, I think. Even with me wearing bright yellow." She held my hand as we walked into knee-deep water, threading our way past cypress knees, and over fallen limbs that threatened to trip us with every step.

"I got lonesome back there by myself, so I started to follow you. That's when I first heard the plane," Margaret said. "The minute I could tell that it wasn't a helicopter, I just knew the same people had come for us again. If we hide here, though, they'll never see us."

"Here I was, thinking you'd try to flag them down. I should have known better. We both thought the same thing didn't we?" I handed her the thermos. "Have some of this, it'll make you feel better." I'd noticed that she wasn't holding her side anymore. There didn't seem to be any fresh blood, either.

She poured a thimbleful in the cup, downed it in one swallow, poured another thimbleful and handed the cup to me. "I think you probably deserve more because of all the running, but you wouldn't take it, would you?" She actually grinned at me as I gulped my mouthful.

"I'm not too thirsty, honest." I wiped my mouth on my sleeve.

"Liar." She replaced the cap. "The ground looks kind of dry over there. Shall we try for it?"

Actually, it wasn't all that much drier, but there was a fallen cypress log for a seat, and it was high enough that our toes cleared the water by half an inch.

"Margaret, if we're going to get out of here, it's going to be up to us. Even if a chopper comes, I'd be afraid it was Scalio's." I was being as straightforward with her as I knew how. "I'm not going to flag down anybody unless I recognize them."

"Then it'll be up to you. I don't know anyone around here — except you, that is. So I'm going to stick to you like glue."

We sat, shoulders touching, listening to the plane as it came closer, then droned away. It was almost hypnotic. There were no other sounds except for crickets and frogs, and a deep bellow that I thought came from an alligator.

Dark clouds began piling up in the west, and the soft daylight that shone into our hideaway began to darken, too.

"Be night in an hour or so, and I don't relish the idea of sitting on this log until daylight." I turned to face her. "You wait here, I'm going to look for a dry place, okay?"

"We'd better go together, don't you think? You could get lost, you know, and if you got lost I'd be lost too." As she slid off the log, her right hand went to her side. The stain had spread.

"Are you still bleeding, Margaret?" I asked, sliding my feet into the water. "Better let me look at your side."

"I'm all right. It oozes a little when I do much moving, but nothing to worry about."

I wasn't too sure about that, but I took her hand and we waded away from the cypress trees, heading east through the swamp. The sound of the plane became fainter, then died altogether.

"Probably running out of gas," I said. "I don't

think they'll be back this late. No use looking for us in the dark." Margaret was hanging on my arm now. I was practically carrying her.

We hadn't found any dry land. At best, the slush was only ankle deep. At its worst, lakes of muddy water were so deep we had to back out and go around. I knew there were snakes, but we hadn't seen any. Our thrashing and splashing had frightened them away, I hoped.

It was almost too dark to see when I stopped. I leaned against a tree trunk, legs too tired to move, and said, "We'd best just sit here in the shallow water until light. I can't see where we're going, and I've gone past tired. One more step through this mud will kill me." I put my arm around Margaret's waist, being careful not to touch the wound, and helped as she lowered herself to the soggy ground.

"Listen," she whispered, clutching my arm. "There's something behind us."

I listened and heard it too. There was a lot of splashing and something was grunting. Something was squealing, too, a high-pitched, frightened sound that ended with a gurgle. Then the swamp was quiet, and the night closed in around us.

CHAPTER 6

The mosquito repellent had been used up with the first few splashes, so now we slapped when they bit. I don't know which one of us had the brilliant idea to cover our heads with Margaret's jacket but if we huddled close together, the jacket kept the buzzing insects at bay.

"It's a good thing that pullover has long sleeves." I told Margaret. "It's thick enough to protect your back and arms." I had no such protection. My jacket was just a thin cover, not good for much except decoration.

We were leaning against a tree trunk, sitting in water, our legs stretched out, our arms in almost constant motion. I had cut a couple of leafy switches, and we used them like a cow uses her tail — splat, splat, from side to side.

"Margaret, why don't you put your head in my lap? You could try to sleep for a little while."

"I can't sleep while I'm wallowing in mud. Anyway, my jacket won't stretch that far." She sighed. "What time is it, do you think?"

Automatically, I held my wrist in front of my face, pretending to peer at my watch through the jacket. My watch, the one with a smashed crystal and no hour hand.

"My watch doesn't know the time anymore. Aren't you wearing one?"

"No. I forgot to put it on this morning. I was anxious to get to the park, and I left it on the bedside table."

Anxious to get to the park to see me this morning? I let it pass, saying instead, "Doesn't morning seem like a million miles away? I was just thinking that breakfast was a long time ago, too. I didn't eat all of my toast, and I regret it now."

"Well, I ate what I thought was enough. If I had known how the day was going to end, I'd have ordered seconds." She sighed again. "Sarah, are we going to get out of here alive?"

"Of course we are. I have a plan, Margaret."

"You mean a plan to have us rescued before we disappear in the mud?"

"Ah," I said. "I'll bet we're out of here tomorrow. You see, I've been thinking . . . and what's come to mind is our way out. You can put money on it."

She sniffed. "I have folding money zipped in my hip pocket, some change too, and I'll hand all of it over if you can get us out of this damn place. It's a considerable sum. You see, I was going to ask you to go to lunch with me, and you looked like you could eat plenty. So I was prepared with a pile of cash. I'll still take you to lunch . . . after your plan works, that is."

I kind of snickered because we were sitting in slush, being systematically eaten alive by mosquitoes, as helpless as any two people could be, and planning a lunch date. I guess it was good to laugh.

"In the morning," I said, "I'm going to follow the compass to a logging road that runs north and south a couple of miles from here. We may have to duck low-flying planes, but if we can find the road, we'll get out."

"We're going to walk out? On a road? How can you be so sure?"

"Listen, I know air rescue, and there's something really funny going on. This swamp should be buzzing with choppers, but we haven't seen anything but that little plane. So, stands to reason they're looking for us in some other place. Only way that could happen is if they were *told* we were somewhere else." I paused for effect, then said, "Margaret, the only other place is the gulf, and it's like looking for a needle in a haystack to search that much water, even for the Coast Guard. The envelope and the basket would float for a while, but they'd go down eventually. There'd be no trace, nothing. How long could you stay afloat without a life jacket?"

"I can swim, of course, but I suppose I'd go down

too. Eventually." Margaret took my hand and squeezed hard. "So what are we going to do?"

"My brother knew I didn't have much gas left. He'd know that we couldn't get far, that I wouldn't go farther than the swamp, anyway. He saw us go straight up, saw us drift over the city toward the swamp. Knowing the winds, and the drift, he'd figure I'd drop just about where we did. I'd never have flown over the gulf, and he knows that."

Margaret squeezed again. "Then why hasn't he come for us," she asked, "or told the other people where to look?"

"I don't know that. But he knows about that logging road. He's waiting for us, Margaret, so we're going to find the road and Lonnie'll be there. You'll see."

"You're trying to make me feel better, and I thank you for that. But, Sarah, that's the biggest crock I've ever heard."

"No," I protested. "Lonnie will be there."

Margaret shook her head. "Tomorrow is too far away for me to think about right now. My immediate concern is that I'm hungry, thirsty, I hurt, and I have to pee."

"I have to go, too. Suppose we get up, do what we have to, then come back to bed. That sound okay to you?"

"I guess," she said, lifting the jacket from our heads. "Let's not come back to this tree, though. What if we keep walking for a while? Maybe there's a dry spot somewhere."

"May I remind you that we're in a swamp. Swamps are covered by water. That's why they're called swamps." I said this while helping her to her feet. She moved stiffly, holding her side. "Put that jacket over your head, girl, or them varmints will eat you alive." I hushed her protest, saying, "Us southern gals are tougher than Yankees. I'll be okay."

A few minutes later we began walking east. At least, I hoped we were moving in that direction. I took her hand. It was so dark under the trees that I couldn't really use the compass. We had to make so many detours around trees and bogs that it was possible we were heading back where we'd started.

After tripping twice over the same submerged limb, I said, "Did I mention that it was night? Did I say that we couldn't see more than ten inches?" I steadied her as she climbed over something sticking partly out of the water.

"I believe you mentioned something like that. A while back you probably said that exact thing a thousand times." She was tiring, moving with effort. "And if you say it again, I'm likely to punch you."

We slogged on, our pace considerably slower now. I knew she was hurting, and I had discovered a few sensitive places here and there that would probably show up as nasty bruises once I could see them. I was thankful that neither of us had broken anything when we came down. We weren't moving fast, but at least we were able to move.

After another hour or so, our progress had almost come to a stop. We were barely lifting our feet, and the darkness was unforgiving. Margaret was gripping my arm, using it for support, her other hand holding her side.

We had stopped talking, concentrating instead on

forward motion, one tiny step at a time. If I could barely move, how hard must it be for her?

"We need to rest, Margaret."

"Not on my account, I hope." But she stopped and slumped against me. I grabbed her with both arms, trying to steady her and not hurt her side.

The jacket had fallen to her shoulders. "Here, let me put this back over your head," I said, "and we'll sit for a while."

She nodded, clearly too exhausted to speak.

I arranged the jacket so that her head and especially her ears and neck were covered. I tied the jacket arms together under her chin. "Now, isn't that better?" She nodded, her hand still clutching my arm for support. "We're going to sit here till daylight." I helped her sit with her back against a tree. "Maybe we can sleep."

I sat down at her side. After a while, I slipped my arm over her shoulders. It was no trouble at all to turn her so that she leaned against me, resting in my arms. I don't think she was even aware that I was holding her. With her head under my chin and most of her body in my lap, I was not comfortable. The ground was soft, though, and she wasn't heavy.

When I opened my eyes it was light, but we were enclosed by a heavy mist. We must have fallen asleep after all, unaware of the white fog that crept through the swamp as nighttime temperatures changed.

Margaret was still resting on me, and my arms were locked around her. She opened her eyes to find my face inches from hers. We stared for a moment, then I said, "Good morning, merry sunshine, how do you feel?"

"It's morning?" She shook her head slightly. "I didn't think I could fall asleep on the ground." She looked around. "From what I can see through the gloom, this looks like where we started yesterday. Did we do all that walking for nothing?"

Her face was flushed. I touched her cheek with the back of my hand. She had fever. "No, we actually walked a couple of miles." No use beating around the bush. "Margaret, you have a fever. I think you're infected from not having any kind of medical attention yesterday, and from the dirty water, and Isis knows whatever else."

She shook her head. "Maybe a little, but I feel all right. When I get to moving around, it'll be okay." Her smile was meant to reassure me.

I eased her off me and creaked to my feet. After stretching, I helped her stand. "I don't think we should travel in this fog, but it'll burn off as the sun comes up. Even if we used the compass to go in the right direction, we couldn't see far enough ahead to avoid places we'd rather not cross."

"How far is the road, do you think?"

"Couple of miles, I guess. Before you woke up, I was sitting there thinking about breakfast. There's gotta be berries or something edible growing around here."

"I didn't see anything yesterday."

"Well, neither did I, but then I wasn't looking for berries yesterday. What I did see was a sassafras tree, and if we had a pot and clean water and fire, we could have tea."

"You mean sassafras like in the old days? Like cowboys used to drink?" Her crystal-blue eyes were bright with fever.

"Yeah, the good guy would strut up to the bar and order a bottle of sassafras. Then, if anybody sneered, he'd shoot them."

"I'd shoot anybody for a drink of anything right now. I'm so thirsty I can hardly talk." She stretched, wincing.

I thought about taking a look at her side. Whatever I saw, there was nothing I could do about it. So instead I said, "I guess we could mosey along, Margaret. We'll just be extra careful, okay. I feel housebound, just standing here."

I took out the compass. East was directly through the tree we'd slept against. I smiled and reached out. She clasped my hand, her smile bravely answering mine. Leading her around the tree, I stepped into the swirling mist.

The fog did lift eventually. There were still pockets of it in low places, but we could see far enough ahead that avoiding deep water was easy. We kept heading east, threading our way between trees, mostly cypress, some swamp willows, a few tupelo gum, a cedar here and there, and others which I couldn't identify. Margaret seemed intrigued by the knobby cypress knees that jutted above the waterline.

"I think they're part of the root system, but I could be wrong. People cut them to make craft things, lamps and stuff."

"I saw some, I think, in a shop in the French Quarter. They were expensive, and they weren't lamps, either, just the wood." She seemed to be walking easier, not exactly bouncing along, but keeping up with my half-slow pace. "I wasn't tempted to buy one."

"What say we rest for a minute." I stared at my feet. "Margaret!" I exclaimed. "We're not standing in water!" Without realizing, we had walked onto solid ground. We were on a tiny island, with pine trees and a spindly oak.

Margaret looked down. "This is the first time I've seen my feet out of water all day. I'm going to sit in that patch of sunlight over there, take off these muddy shoes, and let my feet dry."

I hadn't noticed that the sun was shining. The canopy of trees had effectively blocked most of the warm, bright rays. We sat on the ground, pulled off our shoes and socks, dumped the water and looked at our bare feet. Mine were as wrinkled as dried figs. Margaret's feet hadn't fared any better.

"I know we can't stay till our shoes dry, but doesn't it feel great to have our feet dry, at least? I must have been carrying a gallon of water in each shoe." She examined her feet. "I also have a blister or two that I didn't know about."

"I know these muddy shoes are a pain in the butt," I said, "but they're better than walking barefoot." I was trying to make the best of our situation. Miss Pollyanna, that's me. "You know you're going to have to put those back on in a little while, dry or not."

She wiggled her toes. "Don't be a spoilsport."

I leaned, started to touch her cheek again. She moved her head out of reach.

"Whoa," I said. "I only want to see if you're still feverish. If you are, we'd better camp here for a while. Do you good to rest on dry land." I tried to keep my voice level, neutral, but it was clear to me that she had avoided my touch. I felt my face flush.

"Sarah," she said, catching my hand and pulling me toward her. "I have only a tiny fever, and I am perfectly fine. I don't want you fussing over me anymore." She held my hand to her face. "See? What did I tell you?"

Her face was not overly warm. Maybe a tad, probably not enough to be concerned about.

She pulled me toward her until our faces were very close. "Do you think you could be a little less touchy. I can read your face like a book, Sarah, and you're ready to blow your top again, aren't you? What are you accusing me of this time?"

Remembering Friday, I felt my face positively flame. "I thought you pulled away because you didn't want me to touch you."

She blinked, then shook her head slightly. "I am amazed that you can be so dense. Last night I slept in your arms. You held me as close as two people could get. Did you think I was totally unaware?"

"I was just . . ."

"Just what, Sarah?" She was inching closer, and my heart began thudding.

She let go of my hand, cupped my face, and drew me to her. Then our lips touched and I felt her breath in a soft caress.

"I want you, Sarah. Right here on the hard ground, I want to make love." She was whispering, still holding my face. "If only I had bathed in the last two days, or brushed my teeth, or didn't have this hole in my side, I'd give you an afternoon you wouldn't forget!"

I had a sudden picture of us naked on the sand,

her arms reaching for me. Gulping hard, I managed a choked, "You're gay?"

"I must be."

"You don't know?" I was so turned on, my ears were buzzing. I had instant visions of an unforgettable afternoon. Then, over the pounding of my heart, I heard the unmistakable sound of a helicopter.

CHAPTER 7

We stared at each other as the chopper neared. I was frozen for a moment, then I was on my feet. Indecisive, I stood like a statue until Margaret propelled me towards the edge of our little island where the tree cover was thin and the sky was visible . . . where *we* would be visible.

"No, Margaret," I shouted. "No!" And I pulled back toward the oak tree, dragging her with me.

She fought, arms flailing, and almost broke loose from my grasp.

I pinned her with both arms and hissed, "No, no,

no!" There was no reason not to yell, and I don't know why I didn't. Certainly those in the aircraft couldn't have heard me if I'd screamed my loudest.

I'm fairly strong, but Margaret was almost more than a handful. If she hadn't come to her senses when she did, I don't think I could have held her.

One instant we were wrestling, the next she said quietly, "You can let go, Sarah." And she stood very still while I cautiously relaxed my hold around her. In that moment, the chopper passed almost directly overhead. We flinched, both of us making ourselves as small as possible, huddling against the oak with its thick leaf cover. Neither of us moved until the sound of the motor was far, far away.

"Had I been you," Margaret said, "I would have knocked me silly. I know we didn't want to be seen, just that I forgot for a minute. I was so afraid that they *wouldn't* see us, that . . ."

I interrupted, "It took me a second to remember, too. I can't tell you how much I want to get out of here, Margaret, but I want to get out alive, under my own steam." I put my arms around her, pulled her to me. She did not resist. "There's no guarantee that my brother will be where I told you, that we ever will get out. We just have to keep trying." I was stroking her back, like I would have done a child, and she seemed to melt against me.

"We seem to do a lot of touching, don't we?" Her face was very close, her words a whisper.

"I wouldn't say that," I murmured. "I wouldn't say that at all."

"I slept in your arms last night. Wouldn't you say that was touching?"

"Margaret, there's touching and then there's

touching. I'm holding you now because we're both scared to death and it feels good to be close. Anyway, I thought you were dead to the world last night."

"No, I was aware of you all night long." Her arms slid around my waist. She was pressed against me from my toes to my breasts.

I could have stayed like that for hours, except for the helicopter returning. We could see it through the branches. It was huge and green and menacing. Not to mention loud. As one, we moved to the other side of the oak and huddled against the rush of wind from the whirling blades.

The pilot was making a clean sweep of every inch of swamp, it seemed. The chopper hovered for a long time, not directly overhead, but close. I wanted to make a break and run like hell away from the fury of sound and wind. Instinct kept me glued to Margaret and the oak.

Finally, it was over. They moved to another position west of us, hovering for long minutes as someone, no doubt, scanned the area with binoculars. Even then, we crouched by our tree, taking comfort from the heavy underbrush and the thick, leafy canopy.

"If we move away right now, Margaret, they can't see us from where they are. We'll keep away from places with sunlight, and we'll stay under the trees."

Margaret didn't look too confident, but she nodded slowly.

"I don't want to spend another night floating in this swamp. Do you?" She shook her head no.

"Well, let's go find our road, okay?"

* * * * *

61

Our road proved elusive. But we slogged on, following the compass needle. Once more we ducked the searchers. Very high, and traveling fast, they passed over going northeast, toward New Orleans. When their sound had become too faint to hear, we untangled ourselves from a patch of briars, confirmed our direction with the compass and waded east again.

We couldn't estimate our speed, if you could call it that. We moved cautiously for the most part, avoiding buried limbs that were tangled underfoot, and unseen. I pointed out to Margaret that we were in a cypress swamp, uncut because the trees had not been commercially valuable years ago. East of the highway, the swamp had been cut to the bone many years ago, leaving a vast expanse of nothing, just a sheet of water as far as the eye could see, the surface broken here and there by a stump taller than the rest. We could not have hidden there, unless we stayed completely underwater.

The one attempt to cut this side of the lake had proved too difficult and expensive at the time. The attempt, however, had provided a logging road, the one for which we were heading.

"How could they build a road in a swamp?" she asked. I didn't think she was really curious about the road-building process. She just wanted to talk, and hear an answering voice. The swamp was quiet, our tired sloshing the only sound.

"I think what they did was high technology for its day. I don't know that it could be improved even now. What they'd do is cut trees, shave off the limbs and lay the bare logs side by side in the direction they wanted to go." I used my hands to give her an idea of the process. "Then they sawed thick planks and laid the planks over the logs for the truck tires to roll on. I think they probably secured the planks to the logs somehow, nails or spikes maybe. The road was very stable when it touched land, and it floated over watery areas. I guess they also built turnarounds, else they'd have to back out."

"That so?" Margaret said. "I certainly hope our road is floating somewhere near here. I'm losing steam."

"We're near, Margaret, we're near." Mosquitoes aren't out too much in the daytime, but evening brings them. They were here now, buzzing and biting. I have heard that an effort was made to have the mosquito declared Louisiana's native bird. Isis knows, they were big enough.

"Do you think that truck over there is a mirage, Sarah? The one standing on top of the water." She had stopped wading, was pointing at a truck that was about a block away, resting without apparent support on top of the water.

"No," I said calmly, "that's my brother."

It is to our credit that we didn't rush. Caution was the password for the day, so we crouched on the edge of the tiny pond and scrutinized the truck, the figure in the driver's seat, the surrounding swamp, the floating road as far as we could see, and came to a conclusion.

"You wait here, Margaret, I'll sneak around and get a good look. I think I recognize the truck, but it could be somebody else driving. I just can't tell from here. If it's him, I'll holler. If there's anything at all fishy, I'll come back and we'll try to get the hell out of here without being seen."

On my knees and belly, I inched my way around the pond, keeping out of sight behind the reeds and cattails that grew in the shallows. When I bumped into the mostly submerged road I moved myself hand by hand, using the logs for purchase. I came up on the truck from behind. It was my Lonnie.

"Pssst, pssst." I made as little sound as possible, just enough for him to hear. "Don't move. Stay just like you are," I cautioned. "Are you here alone?"

He looked straight ahead. "I think so, Sarah. Is that other lady with you?"

"We're both here," I said. I wanted to heave myself into his strong arms. "Do you have water?"

"Yes, and some sandwiches. But I don't think it's a good idea to show yourself right now. We should probably wait until after dark. I could have been followed. They may be waiting for you to show yourself."

"That's fine. We'll come after the sun goes down. But could you somehow give me the water. We're dying of thirst."

"I'll put it next to my foot when I get out."

He opened the door and stepped to the road. Casually, he strolled to the other side of the truck. I heard a zipper, then a strong stream of pee hitting the water. I had to cover my mouth to keep from laughing out loud. Certainly the hidden watcher, if there was one, didn't have his attention on the truck at this moment. I slid my arm out of the water, grabbed the jug Lonnie had placed on the plank, and began making my way back to Margaret.

I kept hidden, moving quietly through the shallows. She was crying when I pulled myself out of the mud next to her hiding place in a clump of cattails. Crying so hard, she wasn't even startled by my abrupt appearance. She wasn't making much noise, but I felt her shoulders shaking, her shuddering gulps of air.

"It's okay, it's okay." I tried to calm her. She hugged me, crying even harder. Crying loud enough to be heard, if anybody was listening. "Hush, please hush," I begged.

"What are we going to do now?" She raised her tear-streaked face. "What are we going to do now?"

I could barely understand her. Since I hadn't called her from the truck to say everything was okay, she thought the driver wasn't Lonnie, that whoever was after us was parked where we wanted Lonnie to be. Oh, dear. I shook her gently, mindful of her side, and asked, "Would you like a drink of water?"

Her crying stopped. "A what?" she asked, eyes wide.

I showed her the jug. I held it up proudly. "Water," I said, as if I'd just invented it. "Lonnie gave it to me. He has sandwiches, too, but I couldn't carry them and the water, both."

She reached for the jug. I unscrewed the top and handed it to her, watched her gulp huge mouthfuls.

"He doesn't know if there's anyone else around, so we're going to wait till it's dark before we go to the truck." My own thirst satisfied, I capped the jug and sat it beside me on the mud. Looking at my pants and shirt front, I shook my head. "These things won't ever come clean," I moaned, "I'm mud from head to toe."

Margaret reached for the jug. "When we get back to civilization, I'm going to jump in a washing machine."

"Not if I get to it first," I said.

CHAPTER 8

Waiting was hell. The mosquitoes came out in force. As I sat, swatting and scratching, a sudden picture of elephants in Africa came to me.

"Margaret," I hissed, punching her arm. "Margaret, put mud where your skin isn't covered by clothes. These damn things can't bite through mud!" I heard her skeptical grunt, but she was already scooping up a dripping handful.

We coated mud on our hands and wrists, our necks and faces. "You look like a commando going on a raid." Margaret giggled. She didn't look any better. Only her blue eyes showed.

"Well, it's working isn't it?"

We were shoulder to shoulder, knees drawn up, encircled by cattails, sitting in six inches of mud, our bellies sloshing with water, and each minute brought us closer to rescue. I was less frightened, knowing my huge brother was near. My thoughts turned to the unforgettable afternoon Margaret promised.

Of course, instead of hard, sandy ground, I saw her lying on black silk sheets, her body glowing, her blue eyes misted with desire, waiting for my touch.

That was the only picture, though, just Margaret in bed, waiting. Somehow, I couldn't imagine fitting my body to hers, couldn't conjure the taste of her, or the softness as our bodies merged. Maybe it was because I was smelly and filthy that I couldn't make my fantasy come to life.

Perhaps walking through mud, sitting in mud, being covered by mud, had some deleterious effect on my libido. Whatever, I lost the image after the frame in which Margaret reached for me. I took her muddy hand. "Only a little while and it'll be dark enough to get to the truck. You'll have to kind of slide through the mud like I did, so's not to be too obvious. Make like an alligator, you hear."

"I'll try, I'll try." She dribbled more mud on our clasped hands. "After we get out of this swamp, what then, Sarah?"

Margaret was the law person. She should know better than I did what we needed to do when we reached civilization. High on my list of priorities were questions concerning our rescue, or lack of one. My feeling was that we should immediately run screaming to the police, the FBI, the CIA, the President, and my father, but what did I know?

"You know, don't you," I started, "that I was too far from the House of Detention to be able to identify the shooters. I couldn't even identify Rancatore from that distance. They were all about the size of ants. I saw them being shot, and I saw them fall, but that's about it. The whodunit completely escapes me."

"You're not a very good witness, Sarah. I identified Rancatore and Andrew, and I have a good mental picture of the two men who shot at us."

"Let me get this straight. We were sixty feet in the air, at least a hundred feet from the boulevard that separates the jail from the park and you can identify them? Margaret, you've got to be kidding."

"I'm not joking." She shook her head emphatically, making little flakes of mud fly.

"You could have fooled me," I said. "I'll say this, if they're chasing me because they think I saw enough to cause them trouble, they might as well call it off. You saw more than I did. You're the one they should want dead, not me."

"It wouldn't have been hard for them to find out that the person who took the deposition is the pilot of the balloon they're after. That's two strikes right there."

"Of course I took the deposition, but I don't remember what Rancatore said. I didn't listen." Even to my ears, that sounded thin, and Margaret pounced on it right away.

"They can't know what you remember. But they

do know what you heard." She dribbled mud. "I don't think they know who's flying with you."

I studied the ground for a long minute, not ready for any of this. I am being hunted by the biggest crime boss in the South, who will kill both of us when we're caught, and I didn't really see or hear anything that would harm the man. I was an innocent bystander.

A bullfrog grunted in the distance, things splashed in the pond, mosquitoes danced around us in a frenzy, and I could hear Margaret breathing next to my ear.

"What will happen between us, Margaret?" I whispered softly into the fading light, "Can you forget what I said Friday? I have feelings for you. Think we can do something about them?"

"Tell me what you'd like to do."

I turned slightly, but the mud-smeared apparition facing me was the furthest thing from erotic that I'd ever seen. I started to giggle. "What I'd like to do is wash your face."

Her eyes widened, then she guffawed, a sound that broke the stillness like a shot, even though I clamped my hand over her mouth. We held each other, shaking with helpless laughter.

"You look so funny," she gasped. "The creature from hell . . ." This started her again, and it was many minutes before our laughter subsided.

"It's hard to be romantic when we both look like mud pies."

"Don't get me started," I warned. Then I pushed myself to a standing position. "Here, let me help you up."

"But what about —"

"Don't worry. Anybody looking for us would have homed in on all the noise we just made. And if there was anybody out there, we'd be sieves by now. Let's go get in the truck. Lonnie has sandwiches."

We sloshed and slid our way around the pond. Lonnie hauled us from the water, lifting us to the road. I wiped my mud-smeared hands on my pants, wiped the mud from around my mouth with my hands, and tore the wrapping from a ham and cheese. "I have never in my life tasted anything better," I announced through a mouthful.

Lonnie had already turned the truck around and was cautiously headed for the long-abandoned gravel road that skirted the swamp. It seemed like we were riding on water, the floating roadway sinking under our weight. When I felt the road sag beneath us, I also felt Margaret's hand squeeze mine. She was afraid too.

We lumbered cautiously over the roadway which was now edging dry land. When I felt our wheels catch in the gravel that separated the logs from the paved roadway, I said, "We need to get to a hospital. Margaret's been shot." In other words, now that we're on dry land, let's get moving.

"Why didn't you say so?" Lonnie's careful driving became a headlong race. Ignoring obstructions, he flew us over, around and through a million weed-filled potholes. The Old Swamp Road, as it was mostly called, was in the state of disrepair familiar to Louisiana motorists. We crashed into one chasm, missed the next one by a hair, and soared high over a fallen limb, spewing gravel as we bounced back to earth, wheels churning.

My teeth clenched to keep from biting through my tongue, I asked, "Whose truck? I thought I recognized it."

"Reggie's. I didn't want to use yours, and didn't think it was a good idea to use mine, either." He banged the steering wheel with his fist. "Honey, we didn't put this mess together until last night. There were so many stories going around that we couldn't make heads or tails. Mabel talked to Dad and he called in some markers, I guess."

I clung to Margaret's hand. "My father is a judge across the lake," I said by way of explanation. "He can get information even when there isn't any."

"Do you know why it took a day and a half to get to us?" Margaret was tucked under my arm like a baby chick. I felt her warmth through the muddy jacket. Her thigh pressed mine.

"Sure. First thing I told Rescue was that you went down in the swamp. It was the only way to figure, what with being out of gas and the wind blowing in that direction. Sarah, they probably had choppers in the air before you landed, but a radio call gave your position out over the gulf. A positive sighting, they said, so that's where they headed." Lonnie edged across a wooden bridge that had no railings and very little surface. He looked at me and shrugged. "For a while I thought you might be down in the gulf. You could have gone out of your mind in the excitement. It's been known to happen." His sidelong glance wasn't unkind. Brotherly, but not unkind.

"We think we know who made that call," I told

him. "We're pretty sure it was Vinnie Scalio. He had a small plane over the place where we landed, almost before we climbed out of the trees. They shot at us but we hid under trees and bushes so they couldn't see us. Neither of us thought to get the registration numbers, though."

"Oh my God, are you sure they were shooting at you?"

"Do traffic cops give tickets? Damn right we're sure, huh, Margaret?"

Her laughter was fragile. "Yes," she said, nodding. "We're sure."

"Honey," Lonnie growled over the sound of the racing motor and the rattling truck. "We'll have you to the hospital before you know it."

"Won't they know if we go to a hospital? They could be checking for a woman with a gunshot wound. That's what I'd do." Margaret's hand, still black with mud, rested on my thigh. I felt it tense as we crashed over a small tree fallen across the road.

"Of course," he said, "we can't go to a hospital. That's the first place they'd look." His frown, lit by the dash, indicated deep thought.

"Reggie's wife is a nurse. We'll go there."

"I don't know much about bullet wounds, but I can clean the area and bandage it. Enough to hold until you can get to better care. There could very well be tiny slivers of bone hiding under there. That would keep it from healing, make it more painful than it already is."

"Whatever will help," I said. "We'll simply have to

73

get to a hospital as soon as we think it's safe. Is that okay with you, Margaret?" I was sitting on the opposite side of the bed, gulping scalding coffee as I watched, and holding Margaret's hand as Reggie's wife, Thelma, cleaned around the bullet tears, gently wiping the horribly bruised place.

"I'm with you," Margaret said, as a gauze bandage was taped in place on her side. We were both still covered with mud, completely filthy. Our predicament had been explained to Reggie and Thelma. They had offered what help they could, including a bed for the night.

"No," Lonnie said. "If Scalio is still trying for them, I don't want you all in the middle of it. I'll take them to a motel."

"I'm right next door," Lonnie said. "Knock on the wall if you need me." He gave me a most unexpected bear hug. "I'm glad you're okay," he whispered. I had to blink back tears.

Margaret was already lying on top of the bedcover. "Are we alone?" she asked.

I made sure the door was locked, and I secured it with that little chain thing, too. I walked the few steps to the bed. A trail of mud flaked off my clothes and shoes as I moved. I looked down at Margaret and made a motion for her to move over. "Yes, we're alone." Carefully, I sat next to her, and we stared at each other, unspeaking.

Margaret sighed. "There's something I want to do right now."

"What?" I bent a little lower.

"Bathe. I have to bathe."

"What about your bandage? I don't think you're supposed to get it wet."

"I'm going to peel it off and put it on that dresser over there. Then I'm going to take a shower and wash my hair. I'll stick it back on when I'm dry." She wasn't asking permission.

"I'm not sure that's a good idea."

"Good or not, help me get it off." Using my shoulder, she raised herself to a sitting position. "Move, please."

I stood, and she swung her legs to the floor. Raising the pullover, she uncovered the gauze squares. "You unstick me."

Licking my dry lips I asked, "You're certain?" At her nod, I began peeling the tape as gently as I could. She winced a few times, rolled her eyes skyward when the tape stayed stuck despite my attempts to free it, but she didn't make a sound. Finally, it was off. "Okay," I said. "Go for it."

I sat on the edge of the bed, listening to the shower. When I heard her call my name, I was up in a flash, fearing she had fallen.

"What's wrong?" I asked, yanking aside the shower curtain.

Of course she was naked. How else do you take a shower? I stared, unabashed, at her slender body. Taking in the fullness of her breasts, the dark triangle between her legs and the rivulets of mud draining down her thighs, I started laughing. "You're an awful sight, lady."

"Well, I'm doing my best to change that." She handed me the washcloth. "Scrub my back, will you? I can't twist that way right now."

I helped her dry, watched her clean her teeth with the washcloth, then got the bandage and stuck it back in place, trying not to look too much at her smooth skin and soft breasts. Wrapped in a towel she made her way to the bed. Neither of us had anything except our dirty clothes, so she simply dropped the towel and climbed under the covers.

I showered next, taking much longer than usual. Even after washing my hair twice with the tiny bar of soap, it didn't feel clean. So I washed it again.

"Teach me to love you," she whispered.

We were in bed, but not touching. I turned on my side, facing her, and put my hand on her breast. "I'm not so sure you're gay, Margaret." I spoke softly. I wasn't accusing, just explaining. "I think you just want to be fucked by a woman, I've thought that all along. You say the right things, but they don't ring true, like you memorized stuff from a book or something. That made me angry the other day, but now it only makes me sad. And that's a pity because I like you . . . a lot." I could feel her heart beating faster. "But I want to make love to you," I said. "I'm wet from thinking about it."

"If it's wet you want, feel me." She guided my hand. Her pubic hair was soft, her thighs firm. She was dripping with moisture. Her legs opened wider and my hand slid easily to the small, raised organ that throbbed under my touch. I felt her shudder. Her legs moved farther apart.

CHAPTER 9

I am not the most experienced lesbian in the world. I know that. There are probably plenty of ways to make love that I've never heard of. Those first few times in grade school were hardly more than mutual gropings.

Early on, remembering what that "older woman" had once done to me, I wanted to touch my girlfriends between their legs also. Several times I even got my hand down that far, but I didn't have the nerve to poke my finger inside. We did a lot of kissing, and squeezed each others breasts (once they appeared), but nothing serious below the waist.

In senior high, and away at college, things were different. I spent a lot of time on my back, legs spread their widest, learning what a tongue could do down there. I had found *SEX,* but not with pimply, farting boys whose idea of a kiss was to stick their sour tongues down your throat.

After my lover, Jeannie, sailed off into the Florida sunset, I came home to mostly one-night stands. Some of those one-nighters lasted longer, but I had not yet found anyone I really wanted — after the newness of sex wore off, that is.

I have never made love to a woman with a bullet wound, one who is undoubtedly straight as an arrow, who only wants to see how lesbians do it. I do not perform one-woman shows for anybody. I wanted to make love to Margaret because I was as horny as hell, however I got that way, and because I felt a certain warmth for her. A warmth that seemed to be growing.

I wanted to embrace her as I moved my fingers through her wetness. But to do that, I'd have to touch her side. After all, loving is more than fingering someone's clitoris. I needed closeness, I wanted her thigh between my legs, her breasts pressing mine. I wanted to hear her cries of encouragement as her excitement peaked.

"Margaret," I breathed in her ear. "I'm going to move to your other side so I won't hurt you. Move to the center of the bed so I'll have room."

"Yes," she said.

I propped on an elbow. I leaned to take a nipple,

heard her gasp as I bit the hardened flesh. I took in more of her tender breast, sucking and drawing what I could into my mouth. Then, holding her nipple in my teeth, I raised my face, pulling not too gently, and slid my fingers into her as I pulled.

Her long, drawn-out breath caused another rush of wetness between my legs. I withdrew my hand, took her nipple again, reinserted my fingers, and began a slow in-out motion that started her hips moving higher with each thrust of my hand. Her breathing was surely audible all the way to New Orleans. *Now,* I thought, *now* . . .

In a matter of seconds, I lay between her legs. "Wider!" I urged, parting her labia with my thumbs. "Wider!" It is debatable if this was possible, for she had already opened herself completely. "Now raise your hips," I said, and when I felt her lift, I pushed my pillow under her. Her clitoris was waiting between soft, silken walls. I enveloped it with my lips, my tongue stroking, circling, flicking lightly, then harder . . .

Margaret was making sounds but the roaring in my ears eclipsed nearly all but the frantic beat of my own heart. With some difficulty, my fingers entered her again. I had very little room to move my hand, but my mouth was sucking rhythmically. Margaret's wild movements slowed. For one breathless instant, she was completely still, then she thrust forward and held herself pressed to my face. As she did this, the sound she made probably awakened everybody in the motel.

I kept my fingers in her, but moved so that I lay at her side. I snuggled my arm under her neck, my mouth at her ear, my hand still nested between her legs. "Was that enough?" I asked. "I was trying to be very careful so that I didn't hurt you."

"Yes," she said.

"There's more where that came from, Margaret."

"More?" A long pause. "Yes, more."

I went to the bathroom, my inner thighs slippery; I was so aroused that I hurt. Back in the room, I wiped Margaret's face and upper body with a damp cloth. Her eyes were closed, but she was smiling.

As I dried her, I saw that the bandage showed blood. I shrugged. If she wasn't hurting, we'd ignore a little blood. I wanted to gather her in my arms, snuggle her to me, kiss her all over, hear her make that sound again. I was proud of that sound, of causing it. Could I be falling in love with Margaret Paige? I wanted her. And not just for that night.

She hadn't pulled up the covers, so I lay on top of the spread, too. I turned to her, my hand moving down her body, not touching her bandaged side, coming to rest on that silken mound. "More, you said?" I prompted.

"We did kiss. I want you to kiss me."

"I want that, too, but my mouth isn't clean, Margaret. I washed it with soap, I'd probably foam all over you."

"Mine, too. Soap. We'll foam together." She turned to me. I couldn't see her expression, but I knew we were going to kiss. We did. And her mouth took me in. Passion built from my toes to the top of my head. I did taste soap, but it was a clean taste, not foamy at all.

I kissed her mouth without taking my hand from between her legs. I felt moisture gathering, heat building, and I kept my fingers inside her, our tongues the only movement between us. I was still being very careful, trying not to make any moves that pressed her side.

We kissed and kissed, I kept my arm under her neck, holding her. During another kiss that had my toes curling, I felt her hips begin to move. I was half leaning over her, our mouths joined, when her hand pressed mine, urging me to go deeper, and her hips began moving faster.

A thrill coursed through me. My entire body tingled. This was in addition to the excitement that already had me dizzy. Our kisses had aroused her! She wanted me again. I lifted my head.

"Is this the time for more?" I asked.

"If you make me wait any longer, I'll die!"

"Don't want that," I said. And I made love to her again. I hoped that Lonnie, a thin wall away, would think her cries were from pain, that she'd rolled on her injured side. I hoped he'd think that, but to hear her shriek twice was stretching it. Especially if he heard her for the third time not half an hour later.

"Margaret, we shouldn't make so much noise." I was lying on top of her, raised on my elbows, her leg pressed between mine, and I was moving my lower body in rhythm with the movement of her thigh. "No noise." I breathed. "No noise." Then, unexpectedly, I came. And I made noise.

When the spasms subsided, I rolled away from her. We lay side by side, arms touching, both of us puffing like steam locomotives. I don't clearly remember climbing onto her. It was never my intention. I do faintly recall my loud groan of pleasure as our flesh touched, as I crushed her breasts with mine. I believe it was at her urging, but I can't be sure.

We had been making love for hours. I can't remember ever holding back my own pleasure for that length of time. I had never had an orgasm from the touch of a woman's thigh before, either.

"Margaret, I am in love with you."

"Sarah, I am in love with you, too."

"It may have something to do with sex. What do you think?"

"I think you're right. It has something to do with sex." She nodded, I could feel her head move. "Yes, sex," she said.

"Would it hurt if you lay on your side, and put your head on my shoulder? I want to hold you."

"No, it wouldn't hurt. Besides, I have something in mind." She shifted so that I could put my arm under her shoulders, and she leaned into me. I sighed as I felt her move her hand down my body, resting it where my legs parted.

"Open, please," she said.

"You sound like a dentist." I moved my legs apart and felt her fingers dip down and into me. My entire body jerked with the jolt of pleasure I felt as her hand began to move.

"Tell me if I'm doing this right." Her mouth covered mine, and I couldn't speak to tell her that, yes, she was doing it right. Within seconds, I was incapable of intelligent sound. I could only utter groans of pure pleasure that told her more than words could express.

She was groaning, too. Her breathing was escalating at the same rate as mine, and I knew her wild movements must have caused her pain. She was jerking, and I was jerking, we were both moaning, and my climax was seconds away.

There was a knock at the door.

We froze.

"Open up, Sarah, Mabel and Dad are here."

I looked at Margaret, she took her hand from me, I closed my legs.

Light knocking again. "Sarah, wake up, open the door."

Slowly, I sat up. I gathered the rumpled spread and wrapped it around me. Margaret moved to the edge of the bed, pulled up the sheet.

Mabel entered first. She enclosed me in a hug, her arms squeezing, her lips on my cheek. "I'm so glad you're safe, darling," she said. "We've been worried out of our minds." I saw her glance dart to the bed, taking in the cocoon that was sheet-wrapped Margaret. Without a perceptible pause, she stepped to the bed, her hand outstretched. "We've been worried about you, too, Mrs. Paige. We've called your husband, and he'll be here at noon."

It's a good thing my father was holding me in a crushing embrace or I would have fallen to the floor. I tried to turn to look at Margaret, but Lonnie was standing between us.

"We bought clothes at a hardware store. They may not fit, but you'll have something clean to wear." Mabel turned to Lonnie and my father. "You wait outside while they dress, then we can talk."

Lonnie put the bag on the bed. I turned to face Margaret, but found I had nothing to say. I took the clothes Mabel handed me and stalked to the bathroom, slamming the door behind me. Jeans and a plaid shirt. And a pair of men's slippers, all sizes too big. "You're next, Mrs. Paige," I said, with emphasis on the "Mrs."

Margaret's look was imploring, she winced at the "Mrs." "Please don't, Sarah. Please. You don't understand." Her eyes filled with tears. She had not made a move to get up from the bed.

Ignoring Mabel's startled glance, and Margaret's outstretched hand, I tossed the rest of the clothes on the bed. "I'm going to wait outside," I snarled. "Coming, Mabel?"

My father put his arms around me. "You're sure you're all right, Sarah? No gunshot wounds?"

"No, Dad, only mosquito bites." I was so choked I couldn't make conversation. My father would attribute my speechlessness to the ordeal we had suffered. Mabel would know better. She read the appeal in my eyes. Taking my hand, she led me to my father's town car. "Sit in here, Sarah, and tell me what's wrong."

There was no way I could talk about it then. I began to bawl. Cradled in Mabel's loving arms, my heart smashed beyond repair, I wailed.

"It's all right, baby," she crooned, "it'll be okay." But I knew it wouldn't be.

CHAPTER 10

Mabel and Dad each sat on a chair. Margaret and I, not touching, leaned against the bed's headboard. Lonnie sat on the floor, his back against the dresser. "Bring a chair from your room, son."

Lonnie shook his head. "I'm okay, Dad," he said.

Each of us waited for the other to speak. Finally Lonnie looked at me. "I was watching the basket when I saw your knife blade slashing at the tether. I had no idea what had happened, just that you had gone crazy. When you turned on the gas and held it, I knew something had to be wrong. Ragtime went up

85

like a shot, then start drifting west. We didn't have any idea what had happened. I just stood there with my mouth open."

"I was watching from the drink stand," Mabel said. "I could see your heads from that angle, and I saw that Mrs. Paige was holding the gas valve." Mabel sighed. "I saw the tether fall to the ground and Ragtime rising fast, but I didn't know why —"

"You see, we couldn't hear any shooting, there was so much noise around us," Lonnie interrupted. "I knew you didn't have much gas so you didn't have enough lift to get far, and that's when I really started worrying."

"We stood like idiots. I dropped the drinks. Never did pay for them." Mabel was shaking her head. "I ran over to Lonnie, and we watched you drift away."

"Most of the people watching thought your leaving that way was part of the act." Lonnie shrugged. "They had no idea that there was anything wrong. It wasn't until we heard sirens and all the commotion at the prison that we got a glimmer. By then, you were long gone."

"Yes," Mabel added, "I was just standing there, watching you disappear over the horizon, when a policeman began asking me what I'd seen or what I'd heard. I told him that the only thing I'd witnessed was a balloon called Ragtime headed west with two women aboard. He wasn't interested in a balloon. He wanted to know if I'd seen the shooting. 'What shooting?' I asked."

"A cop started asking me about it, too, and when I learned what had happened, I figured out why you'd skedaddled out of there." Lonnie smiled approvingly at me. "I'd of done the same thing."

"Was that when you were shot, Mrs. Paige?" My father's voice carried authority; we all looked at him.

"Yes," Margaret said. Everyone was waiting for more, but Margaret just sat. The silence stretched.

"You were also shot at from the plane Mr. Scalio sent to look for you?" I had heard him called Vinnie, or Scalio, but only my father would call him Mr. Scalio.

Margaret nodded slowly, her eyes on the bedspread.

"What about it, Sarah?" my father asked when it became apparent that Margaret had no more to say.

"Twice," I said, "they shot at us twice. Once right after we'd landed, and again later." I couldn't remember whether it had been the same day or the next. My memories were of greenery, water, mud, and Margaret's hand in mine.

"Both Rancatore and Mr. Turner were killed," my father explained. "There were four men doing the shooting, all four recognized by an inmate who was looking directly down into the courtyard when the shooting took place. He couldn't get a license number because of the angle, but he described the car. The men shooting were known to be in Mr. Scalio's employ."

I started to interrupt, but my father continued, "A guard at the prison, probably hoping for some kind of payment, told Mr. Scalio that Rancatore would be released at noon on Saturday. This man has since disappeared, probably floating downriver at this point."

I remembered Rancatore and the concrete blocks, and the river drop-off. The guard had acted strangely from the first. If I had said something to Mrs. Paige

87

or Andrew, would the outcome have been different? If she had told me about her husband, would the outcome have been different? Outcome, outcome, who's got the outcome?

"Sarah, unfortunately Mr. Scalio needs to destroy the tape you made at the deposition Friday. It and all the copies. It is one of the most important pieces of evidence against him. Also, you were in a position to see the shooting, and are a corroborating witness. As is Mrs. Paige."

"I don't have the tape," I protested. "I was told to make an original only. I didn't make copies because Mrs. Paige and Mr. Turner didn't want copies made. Isn't that right, Mabel?"

"That's what I was told."

"And I'm not a witness to the shooting. I can't identify anybody. Mrs. Paige can do the identifying, though." Did anyone hear the bitterness in my tone?

My father glanced my way, puzzled, then he looked at Margaret who was still staring at the bedspread. "Is that correct, Mrs. Paige?"

She nodded. "Yes," she said.

"Where is the tape, Sarah?"

"Mrs. Paige put it in her hotel safe. At least that's what she told me. It may or may not be there." I didn't have to add that last, and it made my father look at me with a frown.

"Is that so, Mrs. Paige?" I could tell my father was beginning to tire of Margaret's monosyllabic answers. He leaned forward. "Is the tape in the hotel safe?"

Margaret looked up, sighing. "Unless something has happened to it, the tape is still in the safe at the Beauvoir. I believe I can identify two of the men

88

because I was looking down at them when they began shooting at the balloon. The other two were still shooting at ... The other two men weren't facing up." She shifted position, her chin high. "If we're through, I'd like to leave." She moved her arms from her lap and we all looked aghast at the blood on her shirt.

Lonnie jumped up from the floor, my father sprang from the chair, both reaching for Margaret as she swayed. If they had known that the bleeding started because I had fucked her for hours, would they have been so fast to react?

Surely my father knew of my lesbianism. After all these years, all the women, he had to know. With Lonnie, of course, I had been out since college. It just wasn't something we discussed. Neither of them could have any idea that Margaret and I had spent the evening having sex. She was married, after all.

Necessary or not, Lonnie carried Margaret from the room, my father anxiously trailing. Mabel collected our dirty clothes. I dragged behind them, turning out lights.

The dash clock said four-thirty. Lonnie left Reggie's truck at the motel, and he drove my father's big Lincoln like an ambulance. We flew through the darkness, heading for the first hospital on the north shore. My father made a phone call, which I couldn't hear, then he and Lonnie discussed the reason Lonnie was on the logging road waiting for Margaret and me.

I couldn't hear all of their conversation, but I did

hear my father say, "I'll see to it that they're safe." This was comforting. I don't like to have someone shooting at me, and my father can ensure safety when no one else can. He knows everyone on the south shore, the north shore, and points between.

Margaret was slumped in the corner, Mabel's arms shielding her from the constant jolting. We were still on a gravel road adjacent to the highway, that being Lonnie's idea of safety. He was probably right. No one in their right mind would use the road except for the dump truck operators who were stealing the gravel.

I kept to my side of the seat, not looking Margaret's way, trying not to think about her. I knew my father would take care of everything now that he knew what was happening.

It was beginning to get light. I could see Mabel looking at me. She was puzzled; her face showed it. Margaret's eyes were closed, her lips tight. I thought about leaning over to her and saying, "Did I hurt you, honey?" The words the mouse said to the elephant after they'd had sex. But it probably wouldn't have been funny to Margaret, if she even knew the joke. Mabel would recognize it right away.

It was quarter to six when we pulled up at the hospital's emergency entrance. Dad and Lonnie half carried Margaret through the glass doors. Mabel and I stayed in the car. Mabel turned to me. "You and that woman slept together, didn't you?" No one else would have dared ask.

"Well, Mabel, there was only one bed."

"Don't give me that. I want to know what happened. Why you're acting this way."

"Because she didn't tell me she had a husband.

90

She let me make love to her, fall in love with her ..." I started crying again, much to my own surprise.

"Why, Sarah, I've never heard you say that before. Did you really fall in love with her? Is it because you love her that you're being so hateful?" She handed me a Kleenex. "I think you're just tired, my dear, a good night's sleep is what you need."

A car pulled in behind us, and two burly men got out. They looked at the Lincoln, at us in it, then went into the hospital. I clutched Mabel's arm, "Oh, God!" I choked, "they've found us!"

"No, I think the marines have landed, Sarah. I recognize that first man, he's an ex-cop who works for your father. I don't think your Margaret has anything to worry about now."

"She's not my Margaret." I blew my nose.

"Well, we're all set," Lonnie said cheerfully as he slid back into the driver's seat. "Y'all hungry?"

"Wait! Did she ... Why isn't Mrs. Paige coming with us?" I had to know if she was so badly hurt it required a hospital stay. Had I done the hurting, perhaps?

"There was danger of infection, possibly some bone chips floating around in the wound. She'll rest here a while. The two men you saw are to be trusted," he added. "They'll bring Mrs. Paige to my home later, after a doctor has seen her."

"Now that that's settled, let's eat!" Lonnie was barreling down the highway, heading for a brightly lit station with a sign that said "Cafe." I looked at the shirt sleeves that hung down to my ankles, then appealed to Mabel.

"Here," she said. "Let me roll them for you." She adjusted my sleeves, rolling them neatly above my elbow.

"Mabel, while you're at it," my brother said, "do something about her head. Her hair looks like it had a nervous breakdown."

"Shut up," I said.

CHAPTER 11

My father's home is the same as it's always been. I don't think anything but the sheets have been changed in all these years. My room was the same. All my stuff still in place. I flopped on the bed, eyes wide, the ceiling a blank screen on which I played the actions of the last few days. Beginning early Friday morning, the reel fast-forwarded until the moment I closed the motel door. Then I moved toward Margaret in slow motion.

I bathed her, dried her, lay beside her, and knew again the beginnings of her arousal, the moisture, the heat, and the wild motion of her hips straining against me as her hunger built. I saw all of this, felt every movement, tasted her excitement, felt the vibrations as she climaxed in my arms.

She said she'd die if I made her wait. So, on my ceiling screen, I kissed her. Her tongue was velvet, her nipple a hardened bud between my lips, her vulva sweetly swollen for my mouth to encompass. As I watched this dreamy lovemaking take place, I began feeling my own, present need. The slow unfolding became unbearable. So I clicked to normal speed and I fucked her. I put my fingers in her slippery opening and I fucked her. This was not the usual gentle loving. I felt her stretch, her harsh cries urging more.

The image of Margaret, climaxing under my impassioned lovemaking, had aroused me. Her body still, her blue eyes shining, she looked up at me, and I clearly heard her whisper, "I love you, too, Sarah."

"Sarah . . .wake up, Sarah."

Margaret touching my arm? I rolled over and looked up at Mabel.

"Your friend is here, Sarah, and it's time to get up. You can't sleep all afternoon, not with all the excitement. The driveway's lined with cars, there are detectives everywhere, and your father wants you to talk to them. Get up now."

"My friend?" I asked. "She's here?"

"They brought her over a couple of hours ago, and she's fine. The first words out of her mouth were about you. I told her you were resting."

"Where is she?" I wanted to know so I could avoid her.

"In one of the guest rooms at the end of the hall. I think she's probably sleeping. She looked worn out."

That was no surprise. She hadn't slept other than those few hours Saturday night. Sunday night, of course, neither of us had closed our eyes. I ran my hands through my tangled hair. A shower and shampoo were called for.

"Mabel, if today's Monday, we had a deposition this morning."

"I remembered. I had Roby Lane take it. She was free, and glad to have the work. Now get up."

I keep clothes here, so, finally clean and dressed presentably, I went downstairs. Lonnie met me at the door to the study. "I see your hair hasn't recovered."

"Do shut up," I said. "It may be wet but it's probably cleaner than yours."

My father was at his desk. "Come in, Sarah," he said. "We've been waiting to hear your story." Someone moved a chair to my father's side, and I sat, facing the room, and told the nine law officers what had happened since Saturday morning, omitting the part they didn't need to know.

More than anything else, I think they were curious about Lonnie meeting us at the logging road. How had I known he would be there? I gave them my reasoning, which must have parodied what Lonnie told them earlier.

They did have questions. I said we were too scared to note the markings on the small plane, or the markings on the other plane that had fired into the swamp. What I had to say was obviously added to what Margaret must have told them, for they already had notebooks with pages covered by writing, to which they'd add a word or a line as I spoke.

Finally I had told all I remembered, answered what I could. I went to the kitchen for something to eat. Martha, my father's housekeeper, made a turkey sandwich, gave me milk to go with it, and an apple, and suggested that I sit by the lake and swing in the shade as I ate.

"Has everyone eaten," I asked, meaning had Margaret eaten.

"Not yet, but I sent a tray upstairs to our guest," Martha told me. "Now, shoo, I have to prepare a cold lunch for all those men."

I dragged my way to the oak grove, sat swinging slowly and nibbling at the sandwich. Mabel joined me. We didn't talk, just stared at the wind-ripples on the small lake.

Mabel broke the silence. "What are you going to do?"

I didn't have to ask her what she meant. I shook my head. "Mabel, I am totally devastated. I hurt." I threw the last piece of sandwich into the lake for the fish.

"You've only known her a few days. How can this be?"

"I don't know, it just is. I've fallen for her so hard, it's a wonder I'm not bleeding. What hurts the most is that she actually led me on, gave me all kinds of signs, said she loved me, but didn't tell me there was a husband in the wings. We made love..." I don't tell Mabel every little thing, but... "We made love for hours, neither of us could get enough. I thought at first she just wanted to see what it was like with a woman, but she wasn't pretending. It may have been her first time, but she was as turned on as I was."

Mabel patted my hand. "If this business ever has its day in court, you'll have to see her again. As a matter of fact, both of you are at risk until it's over. Even if Scalio is jailed, he can still get to you."

"I don't know why he'd want to, but I'll stay here with Dad, and she can take her chances back in Boston. With her husband."

"This bitterness isn't like you, Sarah." She stared at the lake. "Tell me what you had in mind if not for the husband. What did you want to happen?"

I had to sigh. Thinking about Margaret was painful. "Well, I don't exactly know, I didn't plan everything day to day, just that we loved each other, and would somehow be together. Either I would go to Boston, or she would come here."

"Was any of this discussed with Margaret? Was she aware of your plans?"

"When you put it that way, no. But she said she loved me, and when you love someone you want to be with them. Right?" I looked at Mabel, aware of the weakness of my position. Yes, Margaret had said she loved me, but I don't remember hearing her say she wanted to live with me.

"Oh, Sarah, you're accusing Margaret of deceiving you, and she hasn't done that at all. Maybe she did want to see how it'd be with a woman. Maybe she didn't come right out and say it in so many words, but you suspected it. You told me as much. You didn't have to accommodate her, you know."

I hung my head, stared at the crease in my slacks. "You're right, Mabel, you're absolutely right."

It was a strange afternoon. One car would leave, another would arrive. The drive and the roadway around the house were crammed. I almost felt sorry for Scalio. I sat on the veranda, nodding amiably at the men who climbed the steps and were admitted into the house.

There had been no sign of Margaret. She must have still been sleeping. I went over and over what Mabel had said. Margaret and I had been thrown together in a situation that accentuated whatever slight feelings I'd had for her in the beginning. I wanted her physically, so I credited her with having the same need. Had I made the first move? Had she?

It seemed to me that she had invited lovemaking, had promised it. No, all I really could be sure of was that she had responded with more passion than I expected. This straight woman had erotic depths that I was sure no man had aroused.

Something must have been decided to everyone's satisfaction because our guests began to leave. There was some slight confusion over the right-of-way of so many cars, but they all managed to leave. All but three. The cars remaining were older models, not different in any way from the average.

I found my father in the study, looking out at the lake, finishing a glass of bourbon and water. "This has been quite a day, Sarah." He turned to look at me. "I've mobilized our forces. You should be reasonably protected, you and Mrs. Paige. I don't think Mr. Scalio will make any kind of move against you at this time. He has done crazy things in the past, however."

"Are we both going to stay here?"

"For the time being, yes. I've sensed a conflict, Sarah, is there anything I should know?"

"No, Dad. We just had too much togetherness, I think. It's okay, really."

He accepted this. "She and her husband will share that large room on the second floor. He can only stay for a few days. What about you, do you have clothes?"

"I keep enough here for a week or two, but I'd like to get to New Orleans to see about my apartment and the office. I have to get my appointment book so Mabel and I can cancel some depositions, find someone else to take over for a while."

My father likes it when I show that I'm a responsible businessperson. He nodded. "I'll have someone take you in whenever you like. You might check with Mrs. Paige, see what she needs in the way of clothing."

I had no intention of discussing clothing or anything else with Mrs. Margaret Paige. I'd ask Mabel to do it. With that thought in mind, I went upstairs to my room.

I piled pillows under my head and settled down to wait for supper. I wondered how I'd avoid Margaret. The only way was to eat in my room like a sulking child. I didn't want that. I only wanted to avoid looking at her. I wasn't startled when I heard the familiar soft knock on my door. "Come on in, Mabel."

"It's Margaret," she said as the door opened. "May I come in anyway?"

I sat up, my heart pounding. I didn't know what to say. She sat on the edge of the bed, and we stared at each other. I don't know what my face showed, but she leaned and kissed me. I was so surprised I almost pulled away from her. Almost.

It was a sweet kiss, our lips brushing tenderly, our breathing easy. Then her hands closed on my shoulders and she eased me down on the bed until I was lying on my back. Her hands still clasping my shoulders, she pressed her mouth to mine — not easy, not gentle, but with such passion that I clung to her, my tongue dancing in the hollow of her mouth, her tongue's movement matching mine.

This was morning again, and my ceiling movie was beginning to fast-forward. Margaret unbuckled my belt, I slipped my slacks and briefs down as far as they would go. Margaret's mouth still on mine, she touched me between my legs, and I felt her fingers slide into my vaginal opening. There was no foreplay that I remember. Just our mouths joined, and her fingers moving inside me.

On the ceiling, I saw myself jerking wildly, often dislodging her hand. I watched her move her mouth from mine, press the side of her face against me and frown in concentration over what her hand was doing. Faster and faster. I watched us, Margaret half on top of me, my legs stretched apart, her hand dipping into the dark fuzz and beyond, my mouth tensed in a rictus of pleasure.

Then it was over. She covered my mouth as I

groaned aloud. The reel slowed, my legs relaxed, slowly came together.

"I hate to be interrupted, don't you?" she said. "In my imagination I've done this to you a hundred times today." She laughed quietly, helped me pull up my slacks, straighten my shirt.

I stared up at her, reading her pleasure in those bluest of blue eyes. She leaned to kiss me again.

"Now I want you to do that to me, but we'll have to wait." She saw my glance at the door. "Don't worry, I locked it." Rising, she pulled me to my feet. "We've never really hugged, have we?" We hugged, we kissed some more. "Did I do it to your satisfaction?" she asked. "You'll have to teach me, you know. I may think of some things on my own someday, but for now I'll follow your lead."

She didn't notice that I hadn't said a word.

CHAPTER 12

Martha fed us in the formal dining room. I sat next to Margaret. Her husband, Ralph, who had arrived later than expected, sat directly across the table from me. Our seating arrangement couldn't have been better. It allowed Margaret and me to touch each other under the table. I must have used my napkin three dozen times. Every time I reached for it, I could stroke Margaret's thigh. For long moments, we could even clasp hands. I had watched Ralph lead her into the room, her hand on his arm. He was solicitous of her, I'll say that. He was also gay. I don't know if anyone else saw it, but I knew right away. He held the chair for her and saw to it that she was properly seated, just like a loving husband.

My father, Mabel and Lonnie approved of this. I could see in their faces that they liked the way she clung to his arm, not because she needed support, no. More that she enjoyed touching him, was glad he was here.

A huge weight lifted from my chest, because I knew the kind of touching she enjoyed. When she turned to me, and our eyes met, I almost fell off the chair. There was such naked desire in her glance that I wondered it didn't make noise. My face flushed, and I had to turn away.

Ralph had a deep voice. He also had short, golden-blond hair, a magnificent tan, a three-piece suit, and a ruby pinky ring on his delicate little finger.

"It's good to meet you, Ms. Bodman," he'd said in his throaty purr. "My wife has told me so much about you."

I'll bet she has, I'll just bet she has. "Please call me Sarah, Ralph," I said in my smoothest tone.

"Of course, Sarah it is." He smiled to show his perfect teeth. I had smiled back to show my perfect teeth also.

There was a mutual admiration between us, I knew he was gay, and I felt that he knew I was a flaming lesbian, one who had "had" his wife, and more than once from the look of us. His wife's hand was, at that moment, climbing up my thigh.

Dinner was a smashing success. Ralph was also a lawyer, so he and my father could talk the same language. Margaret, though she knew the jargon too, was too busy with her napkin to join their conversation. Thank goodness they didn't talk about Vinnie Scalio.

Martha kept our plates filled with her superb cuisine, some kind of delicately seasoned fowl. I recognized wings and tiny drumsticks. I saw that Margaret didn't touch her wine. I was glad because I don't like wine, neither the Saturday night special nor the stuff from my father's dusty bottles.

I'll take a little beer with seafood, but that's the extent of it. In Florida, Jeannie became addicted to the harder stuff. She'd have three glasses to my one, be too hung over the next day to do any diving. I never did understand why.

Stuffed to the burping point, I folded my napkin. "Walk with me to the lake," I said to Margaret. "I think you'll like standing on dry ground, looking at the water instead of sinking in it knee deep. How about it?"

Margaret looked at Ralph, raised her eyebrows in question.

Assuming that the invitation included him, which it hadn't, Ralph said smoothly, "You two go ahead. I think I'd rather stay inside."

My father approved of this, too. He would take Ralph and Lonnie to the study and they'd have a glass of something mellow.

"Want me to go with you?" Lonnie asked me.

"We'll be okay," I said. I thought he was being funny, then I remembered Scalio, and the guards who were sure to be crawling all over. Margaret and I wouldn't be alone, after all. I pushed back from the table, turned to Margaret. "I didn't think to ask if you were too tired for a hike. Would you rather come to my room and watch TV?"

"I'd like that," Margaret said quietly. "I am rather tired."

I made sure the door was locked. "We have to talk," I said when we stopped kissing long enough to breathe.

"We do?"

"Yes," I managed to say before her mouth covered mine again.

Kissing became touching. Kissing and touching led to feeling soft private parts. "Do we take turns?" she asked. "Who does what first, or does it matter?"

"Margaret, you honestly don't know?"

"Sunday, when we made love, you satisfied me first. Several times, as I remember. Then I made love to you, but I didn't get to finish that until today. I'm not being funny, Sarah. I don't know whether to fall on my back or push you down onto yours."

"Well, we don't take numbers, if that's what you mean. We, ah, engage in foreplay, like we're doing. We touch, and we kiss, and we kind of roll around on each other. Usually, we undress."

I had to clear my throat. "I'll touch you, lick, bite, whatever, and you'll do the same to me . . . then whatever happens, happens. I don't know who decides."

"You're frowning, Sarah. Don't lesbians talk about sex?"

"Of course. It's just that I've never had to explain who does what. As a group, we aren't very organized,

don't even have a manual or a navy that I know of."
I cleared my throat again. "I think I'm embarrassed."

"Sarah, I have never touched a woman sexually
before. You're the first. Ralph and I, well, we . . ."

"Don't say anymore. Suppose we undress, and
we'll see."

Naked, she was more beautiful than I
remembered. The bandage on her side wasn't big. It
was more sexy than anything else, I thought.

"Now, let's kiss." I lay on her, my legs between
hers, and I held her face and kissed her mouth, her
eyes, slipped my tongue in her ear, then licked the
other ear. She tried to catch my lips with hers. A
good start. She squeezed my buttocks and began
pulling me into her, lifting her hips at the same
time. Another good start.

I propped myself up and offered her a breast. Her
hands came up like a shot and she claimed both
breasts, sucked both nipples and teased with her
tongue, her teeth finally closing on one, causing me
to cry out with both pain and pleasure.

I fell on her again. My breasts, wet from her
mouth, pressed into hers. My breathing was loud.
Hers was louder.

"Are you taking notes?" I asked.

Her laugh was more like a grunt. With strength I
didn't know she had, she flipped me onto my back,
felt between my legs and whispered in my ear, "I
think your number's up."

I knew it was. She moved down my body. I felt
the pillow slip under my rear end, then she put her
mouth on me. I have never been so wet. I could feel
liquid simply pouring from me, and I have never had
an orgasm as prolonged.

"I see what you mean," she said when my body stilled. "It just happened, didn't it? I don't know at what instant my need to love you became so strong I had to have you . . . I had to fuck you." She sounded very proud at using the f-word.

"And you did it beautifully," I whispered. "Let's see if I can do as well."

"Let's talk, Margaret." We were still naked on the bed.

"You were angry, weren't you? About Ralph, I mean. I could see it in your face. You have the most adorable scowl." Her head was on my shoulder, her body snuggled against me, one hand free to caress my breasts.

It was hard for me to concentrate, I felt heat building as she stroked. Didn't she know that there was no way I could do any serious talking while she was stimulating my mammary glands? I don't believe she was trying for any particular effect. She just hadn't known that another woman's breasts could be so interesting. Also she was watching my nipples harden as she rolled first one then the other between her fingers.

"Margaret, let's be serious for a minute." I took her hand in mine. "Ralph is gay, isn't he?" It doesn't hurt to get to the point. Margaret did it, why shouldn't I?

For a minute she didn't answer. She probably hadn't discussed this with many people, I thought. It wasn't the kind of thing you advertised.

She took a deep breath. "We were in law school

together. I dated, but there wasn't any pleasure in it for me. I even slept with a couple of boys in the class, experimenting. That was even worse, and I became a sort of loner." She pulled her hand from mine, gently touched my face. "In high school, I was strongly attracted to one of my teachers. She was young, obviously not very experienced with teacher-pupil interactions. She would hug me, all very casual. One day, she kissed me. Someone saw us, and she was dismissed. I didn't become close with anyone else after that. I was afraid to make friends."

I kissed her fingers and listened.

"In law school, Ralph asked me for a date. He was a senior, and five years older. We got along just fine, I enjoyed being with him. I felt no strain at all, and he didn't press me to have sex." She giggled, a very un-Margaret like sound. She touched my nose, "Not at all like you."

Her fingers moved to my lips, and I kissed each one as she touched my mouth.

"We married when he graduated. I finished and went to work for one of Boston's legal programs to help the indigent. Ralph and I tried sex at first. I thought we had to, and he thought he ought to. It was a disaster. Neither of us enjoyed it."

Her fingers were parting my lips, slowly entering my mouth. I began sucking each finger in turn. Then she inserted two fingers, drew them part way out, gently eased them in again.

"Do you know what this feels like?" she asked as she continued the movement.

"Uh huh." This was the only sound available to me. It didn't take a Philadelphia lawyer to figure what was happening. It was, after all, a Boston lawyer making it happen.

"Have we waited long enough?"

"Uh huh," I answered.

Some time later we dressed, and Margaret left. I straightened the bed, trying in vain to get the sheets tucked in properly. Martha would think I'd had nightmares of gigantic proportions. I wondered that we hadn't ripped the mattress cover.

I was resting on the chaise, picturing my beautiful, lost Ragtime and thinking that we still hadn't talked about what was important, when I heard a soft knock. It was Mabel.

"I waited for Margaret to leave," she said. I had the grace to blush. She sat next to me. "Do you know what you're doing?"

Mabel has been mother, confidante and friend for almost all of my life. She loves me. There was honest concern in her soft, brown eyes. She would not interfere, but wanted to make sure I didn't fly away without some direction in mind.

"Of course I know what I'm doing." *I am fucking Margaret every chance I get, that's what I'm doing. And she is taking good care of me, too.*

"I don't want you to get hurt, Sarah. She's married, after all."

"Her marriage is a farce," I said. "He's gay, if you hadn't noticed."

"Well, what does that mean in apples and oranges? She's still married."

"We haven't worked it out, Mabel. But we will." I didn't have an inkling how we'd do this, but I knew what I wanted.

"All right, dear, just be careful." She patted my hand. "In the morning I'm going to New Orleans to get our appointment book. Do you want to come along?"

"Why not?" I said. "What time?"

"I'd like to leave right after breakfast. I have some birthday shopping to do, and I think I'll find what I want on Canal Street."

"Sure. Last Friday I was going to take Margaret for some boudin, but we didn't get to go. Will it be okay if she comes with us tomorrow?"

"Certainly. But you remember, don't you, that there'll be an escort? Your father insists that you be driven wherever you go, and two of his men are to be with you at all times." She patted my hand again. "So, if you had any plans, forget them. You and Margaret won't be alone."

I scowled. "Mabel, I truly love her."

"Of course you do. She's a very likable person. If I sound tentative, it's because you haven't known her very long. You knew Jeannie much longer, remember? You also 'truly' loved Jeannie."

Drat! Mabel never forgot anything. To reassure her I said, "Jeannie and I were very young, Mabel. I'm older, more experienced now, and I know what I want. I can take care of myself, you'll see."

Mabel turned very serious. "Sarah, don't hurt Margaret. She seems very self-assured, almost formidable, but I sense that she's more vulnerable than you realize. Give her time to grow into this, don't force her if she's not ready."

110

"I haven't forced her into anything yet. I don't know that I could." Sex with Margaret was a thing of mutual delight. I hadn't forced her at all. Taught her a few moves maybe, but nothing that she didn't want to learn.

Mabel was having the last word. "You're like a freight train, running over everything in your path. Just don't run over Margaret, please."

"I won't, I promise."

Mabel put her arms around me. We hugged and she kissed my cheek. "Keep your promise, darling."

CHAPTER 13

I was up early, finally having gotten enough sleep. Margaret ate in the kitchen with me. Her appetite matched mine. We sat over coffee, waiting for Mabel to finish her breakfast, then we were escorted to one of the unremarkable sedans parked in the drive. And I do mean escorted. It took two men to get us to the car. They got in after we were seated.

They didn't introduce themselves, so neither did we. Margaret sat in the middle, and I held her hand. She was not too sure about this, and she glanced at Mabel, then at me, her eyes questioning. I smiled and squeezed, taking no notice of Mabel who was studiously looking out the window. From the front seat, they couldn't see us unless they turned around, so Margaret settled in, her hand warm and soft in mine.

We drove across the causeway, Margaret asking questions about Lake Ponchartrain and the double roadway that spans it. In no time, it seemed, we were nearing the river and Esplanade Avenue. There wasn't a parking spot near where I live, and the two men wouldn't let us out in front of the building, but drove around until they found a vacant curb. Then, one walking in front and one in back, they led us across the broad esplanade to my door.

We went up the outside stairs like that, single file. The short one opened the house door, scrutinized the hall, then held the door for us to enter. I knew there was something wrong when I looked at my door. It was ajar. Both men saw it, too, and they moved us back to the steps, then cautiously pushed my door open. Each man suddenly had a gun.

They were inside for only a minute. Mabel, Margaret and I were clutching one another, expecting shots to ring out. When the men emerged, they motioned us inside, and they were frowning. I soon saw why.

My apartment had been trashed. The furniture was in pieces, upholstery slashed, everything breakable broken, the walls spray-painted. I walked into the bedroom, and there was nothing that hadn't been ruined. My clothes were in shreds. Even the curtains drooped in ragged pieces. They must have used an axe on the bathroom fixtures, the porcelain was cracked and broken beyond repair, the plumbing ripped out, the tile floor smashed. In the kitchen there was not one pot, pan, dish or cup that hadn't been broken. Even the microwave door had been broken off. They had taken the picture of my mother from the bedroom wall, shredded it into pieces and spray-painted the scraps.

I couldn't sit down to cry. There wasn't anything to sit on.

What furniture I had was slashed, legs broken off, paint covering what little upholstery was left clinging to the frames. The two men stood in the doorway, trying not to watch as I bawled, standing in the middle of the room beneath the broken light fixture. My feet crunched glass with every move.

"Please don't cry." Margaret was sobbing too. "We'll buy everything new, it'll be all right. Please." We were holding each other, but it was okay to cling under the circumstances.

"Miss, there's nothing you can do here, we'd better take you back across the lake." This was from the short one, but both faces held sympathy. I bawled louder.

The tall man said, "Looks like they came in over the balcony, broke their way in through the French doors. We can try for fingerprints." His shrug said it would be a waste of time, though I knew it was standard procedure once I had filed a report.

"My video equipment..." I looked around, my rolling stand and everything on it was gone! Everything in my apartment had been trashed, but the video and audio equipment had been taken. And, if they had been here, what was to stop them from trashing my office?

"We have to check my office." I looked around wildly, it was like standing in a pile of garbage. "Please, please, please take me to my office."

I sniffed all the way to Magazine Street. The tall man asked me to wait in the car while he went inside, but I was out and crossing the sidewalk before he finished talking. I should have listened to him. My tiny office was, if anything, in worse shape than the apartment. I stood in the doorway, surveying the ruins. Margaret came up behind me, Mabel behind her. I was past crying. I looked at them and said, "Let's get to the Beauvoir."

There were five solemn faces riding up in the elevator. Margaret's room had a "Do Not Disturb" sign on the door. All five of us knew what we'd see when the door was opened. And we saw just what we thought we'd see. Her curtains were in shreds, too, along with the mattress, the chair, and even the rug. Her clothes and shoes were slashed. There was nothing recognizable in the room.

"I've already cried myself out over your things, Sarah, so let's get the hell away from this mess," Margaret said. "I've lost nothing of value here."

"Don't you want to get something from downstairs, Margaret?" I was remembering the tape.

"Probably be safer at your father's place, wouldn't it? All right, let's go." We left the "Do Not Disturb" sign on the door, so that the police could examine the room before the hotel personnel could start their renovations.

It took only a minute to get the tape, the desk clerk friendly and obliging.

"If I drank," Mabel said, as we left the hotel, "I'd

115

take one on right now. I'm so shocked I can't think straight. Does anybody know what we do about this?"

"We get back across the lake," the tall man said. And that's what we did.

My father was furious. There was a line of white around his lips from clamping his mouth together. He hugged me and I began crying again. We were all in the study waiting for the police. Ralph was holding Margaret's hand, his chair pulled close to hers. Mabel and Lonnie were on the couch, Martha was in the doorway wringing her hands.

"We'll replace everything, Sarah," my father was saying. "Don't worry, we'll get it all back like new." He never could stand to see me cry.

I didn't want it back like new. I liked my apartment the way it was. I wanted it back the way it was. I knew, and everyone in the room knew, that it could never be the same.

"Why me?" I wailed, "I didn't do anything to that man."

"Sarah, I will take care of it." My father said this firmly, his tone convincing.

A sudden thought flashed. "My car, what happened to my car?" I looked around at the startled faces. "Where's my car?"

"I have your car, Sarah. It's safe in my driveway. That and your truck." These were the first words Lonnie had spoken since we walked into the room. He wasn't much on showing affection, couldn't stand weeping women either, but he was quick to take action when it was called for. I should have known he'd remember my car.

Two law officers arrived, both from Orleans Parish. I gave a statement and answered their questions. They knew about my balloon and Vinnie Scalio and the murders on the courthouse steps.

"You're insured?"

I nodded, thankful that I'd struggled to pay the premiums.

That seemed to do it. They closed their notebooks and left.

"You haven't eaten," Martha announced from the doorway after they'd gone. "I've fixed a buffet. Drinks are on the porch. Everyone come eat."

We trailed her to the dining room, filled our plates. I didn't think I could eat, but I did. When anyone would glance my way, they'd smile sympathetically. All but my father. He had come to a decision, it seemed, and was no longer troubled about the events of the day. I wondered what it was he had decided.

"Your furniture, the video equipment, all these are just things that can easily be replaced," he said.

Lonnie had a stack of newspapers to show Margaret and me. We were in the headlines. We read, BALLOON LOST OVER OCEAN and WOMEN TRY FOR GULF CROSSING. We had to laugh. There seemed to be no connection between the balloon and the shooting. Not at first. One enterprising paper, a local supermarket weekly, announced that two women, they gave only my name, had killed two men on the steps of the House of Detention. There was no mention of Vinnie Scalio.

Apparently, Margaret and I had leaned out of the balloon, shot two men, then floated away to be seen no more. MYSTERY BALLOON IN FATAL SHOOTING. The mystery was where they got their misinformation.

The most recent daily had an inch or two on a back page, stating that air rescue had located the missing balloon and the passengers were rescued unhurt. So much for the credibility of the press.

Lonnie asked Mabel why she wasn't worried about her own apartment.

"I have family coming up through the floorboards. If my place had been trashed, the trashers would be in more pieces than the furniture. My family hasn't called, so I know everything's fine." Mabel's smile was grim. "I'd like for a couple of my nephews to get their hands on the men who did this to Sarah."

I nodded emphatically. Mabel's nephews worked on the dock. They could probably mobilize an army if they needed one.

During a lull in the conversation, Ralph made an announcement. "My office called. The date's been moved up on an important case. I have to be in Boston tomorrow morning. I wouldn't have considered going back, except that you're in good hands." He gazed fondly into Margaret's eyes. "And you're mending physically."

"Oh, dear," Margaret said. "I don't think it would be wise for me to leave now. There's too much unfinished."

"I wouldn't hear of your leaving. You've been given an extended leave. I talked with your office this morning, too. Take whatever time you need to get this cleared up." He looked at my father. "If we may impose on your hospitality . . . ?"

"You're certainly welcome to stay here as long as it takes, Mrs. Paige."

Yes, I said to myself, yes, yes, yes!

Ralph needed transportation to the airport. He had managed a seat on the eleven-forty that changed in Atlanta. We decided to go to the airport with him. I, for one, wanted to be sure he didn't miss the plane. So Ralph, Margaret, my father, my brother and me in the town car, escorted by a sedan with two men, and followed by a sedan with two men, paraded across the causeway, merged with the I-10 interstate, and soon rolled to a smooth stop on Moisant's passenger dock.

Margaret and Ralph embraced. I didn't look. Margaret returned to sit at my side. I looked. I took her hand in mine.

"We will have the whole night together," I whispered.

"Yes, I know." Her hand tightened. "A whole night with no interruptions. I will have you for the entire night."

Have me she did. I also "had" her. Our lovemaking was gentle, our kisses tender, the final surge of passion sharp, frenzied, and deeply satisfying.

"Am I a one-night stand?" she asked.

"If you are, I want the night to last forever. I love you, Margaret. I love you now and for always."

"I'll bet you say that to all your one-nighters."

119

She was cradled in my arms, her softness pressed against me. "I know I'm not your first," she said sadly. "I wish I could have been."

"Why in the world would you? Just think, if I hadn't known what to do, we'd never have gotten this far. You were saying the right things, but you weren't saying them at the right time. I was turned off, for the most part. If you hadn't been so damn sexy, and me so horny for you, you'd be on that plane for Boston right now."

"You were horny for me?"

"How could you not know that? I wasn't that way at first, but it grew on me. You grew on me. In the motel I almost couldn't breathe for wanting you."

"Me too. But I was afraid I'd do the wrong thing, that you wouldn't find me desirable. I wanted to be desirable for you. And I was so . . . so unwashed."

"Margaret, I think I desired you that day in the prison."

"Speaking of desire . . ."

"Again?"

"Um."

Morning came too soon. I woke to find Margaret's blue eyes half open, sleepy, and looking at me.

"I've been awake for a while," she said softly. "I didn't want to wake you. You were sleeping so soundly, snoring so sweetly." This last was said with a little half smile, her eyebrows raised. I yawned, stretched, blinked my eyes wide. I felt sticky all over.

Sticky from me and sticky from Margaret. "I'm going to shower, okay?"

I had soaped all over, was trying to keep my hair dry, when Margaret pulled the curtain aside. "I have to tell you something."

"You have to tell me now?" It was okay with me, but bed was a better place to have a conversation.

She pulled down the toilet seat and sat. "Yes, now." I waited for her to say whatever it was, but I wasn't alarmed.

I was splashing her, so I said, "Can you tell me through the curtain, or would you like to get in here with me?" She was naked. All she had to do was step into the tub.

She closed the curtain. "Sarah." Her voice was so very serious, "I've been dishonest with you."

My mind clicked to dead slow. "Dishonest?" I asked, my thoughts a blur. "Dishonest?" I asked again. "About what?"

"You are not the first. I fell in love with a secretary in my office. It was the first time I had ever felt that way about a woman, the first time I had wanted to . . . to touch a woman. I told Ralph. He said to go for it, said he had known it would happen some day. I didn't tell her, of course. She was, and is, completely unaware of my feelings, but I was miserable. I couldn't even stay in the same room with her."

I had stopped rinsing. "When was this?"

"Now. It still is." I pulled the curtain aside. Her hands were clasped, head bowed, shoulders slumped.

"You're in love with this person?" I was confused.

121

"Well, no, not now. But that's why I was so forward with you. I knew you were a lesbian. It was there in black and white. I thought I was, too, and Ralph said I'd never know if I didn't try, so I wanted to try with you."

"You led me on!" I hooted. "You were out to get me all along. I was to be a sample." I grabbed a towel. "Damned if I didn't think you were reading lines you'd memorized from a Naiad quickie. And you were, you really were!"

She didn't speak.

I knelt in front of her. Lifted her chin. "My darling," I said as clearly as I could, "I love you even more for your honesty. It's okay if you have feelings for some secretary. Feelings are normal. Just don't share yourself with anyone but me." Her tears started to flow. I kissed them away, helped her up from the seat. "Now that your conscience is clear, take a shower, then come back to bed."

"You're not angry?" She stepped into the tub, my ivory statue, my Boston baby, my love.

"No, not angry at all," I said seriously, closing the curtain so she wouldn't see my happiness and mistake it for amusement. Back in the bedroom I straightened the bedclothes, plumped the pillows, lay down naked and waited. She was not long in coming. Not long at all.

CHAPTER 14

"I'm going home for a while. I still have a birthday gift to buy. If you'd like to come to the mall with me, I'd welcome the company."

Margaret and I looked at each other. Margaret shrugged. It was okay with her as long as we'd be together.

"I don't think so, Mabel. I want to get the trash cleaned out of my apartment, whatever we can do with a broom. Martha has called a cleaning lady, and Margaret and I can sort through things and make piles of stuff to be taken away later. Why don't you come on by when you've finished shopping?"

"Maybe I will. I intend to take care of the office tomorrow. My oldest niece will be free, and she'll help. We need to have the phone connected and . . . well, you know what's to be done."

Yes, I knew how big a mess the office was, and I was glad Mabel wanted to clean it. I thought Margaret and I would do a little cleanup at the apartment, finally get to eat the boudin I had promised, maybe look at furniture. Who knew what we might do? There was a whole day of being together like regular people. Except for the two men who tagged our every step, that is.

My apartment looked worse than I remembered. Tears stung my eyes as I surveyed the wreck. Grimy fingerprint powder filming everything. Margaret put her arm around my waist, unmindful of the two men looking on. She was shaking her head in disbelief.

"Do you have a broom?" she asked.

"It's over there, broken, of course. But there's a closet in the hall with cleaning things. We can use whatever we find."

The tall man sat in the hall on a kitchen chair with a broken back watching the front door. The shorter one leaned against the balcony rail. He was watching the street and the patio. They didn't offer to help, but they weren't being paid to help me clean.

Having piled most of the larger pieces in a corner, we were emptying things we could sweep into a large trash can we'd found in the hall closet. I was bent over, pushing scraps with a dust pan when I heard one of our bodyguards say, "You can't go in there, Miss."

I didn't look up. It hadn't occurred to me that a woman could be a hired killer, sent to get us in broad daylight. Could it be the cleaning lady Martha sent? I finished pushing a few more scraps into the pile.

"My God, that must have been some party, Sarah."

I froze. Leaning over a pile of trash, I wasn't even able to straighten up. I was aware of the tall man in the doorway, and a slim figure in a skirt standing in front of me, and of Margaret, who had stopped sweeping, watching.

It seemed to take hours for my knees to unbend. "Hello, Jeannie," I said, rising to my full height, dustpan still dangling from my hand. "What brings you to this neck of the woods?"

"I thought I'd say hello. Freddie and I are in town to look at some property, and I didn't think you'd mind if I came by." She darted a shy glance at Margaret, then looked back at me. "I'll go if you want me to."

"No, it's okay. I'm glad to see you." I was glad to see her. When she left I'd been heartbroken, then I got mad, but now I wasn't anything. She was just someone I had once known. I motioned for Margaret. "Jeannie's an old friend from Florida," I said. "Actually, we were in school together." They smiled at each other. "Margaret is from Boston, here on business."

Margaret held out her hand. "Nice to meet you, Jeannie."

I hadn't told Margaret about Jeannie, that we had once been lovers, and Margaret's smile was open, friendly. Jeannie smiled back, but in her eyes there was instant recognition. She knew Margaret and I were more than casual friends.

"I called Lonnie to find you. You're in the phone book, but both of your phones seemed to be out of order." She looked around again. "Now I see why. What in the world happened, Sarah? Looks like a hurricane hit."

"Didn't Lonnie tell you?"

"Tell me what? He did say that you crashed your balloon, but that you weren't hurt. I was sorry to hear it. I know how much you always loved flying."

Jeannie and I used to lie on the beach, watching the birds and the waves, and I'd talk about flying, about getting my own balloon someday. We'd draw designs in the sand, plan the colors, the size, and the merits of a round versus a square gondola. Jeannie remembered those slow, easy hours, too. I could see it in her eyes.

"There's more to it than what Lonnie told you. Margaret and I shared a real adventure. We should write a book, huh, Margaret?"

"Lonnie said something about you getting shot. Did that really happen?" Jeannie asked Margaret. "Or was he kidding as usual? I never could tell."

"No." Margaret touched her side, "I was grazed, not really hurt. It didn't amount to much, but Sarah thought it did."

Seeing that Jeannie didn't pose a threat, our tall guard had gone back into the hall but now he appeared in the doorway with a young woman.

"I'm here to help with the cleaning. Miss Martha sent me." I was happy to see she had a plastic bag filled with broom, mop, bucket, and gloves.

"Come in, we can certainly use your help."

Jeannie pitched in, stacking broken tiles in the bathroom, and we moved the mess around for another couple of hours. Mostly things were in heaps. Some paper, some broken crockery, pieces of wood, scraps of bedding, curtains, chair parts and couch upholstery. Each had its own pile.

"What I need is a truck under the balcony. We could just push everything over the edge, make a clean sweep." I took a deep breath, to hold back more tears. "I have to start over, y'all. I need plumbers, carpenters, electricians, painters ... Hell, I need a new apartment!"

Margaret was sensible. "Why don't you move?"

I surveyed my spray-painted kitchen. "I own the place, that's why, and I'm too poor to pay rent."

"Speaking of poor ..." Jeannie gestured. "Are those two men getting paid for standing around? They aren't doing anything that I can see."

"My father hired them to keep Margaret and me safe. He's paying them, I hope." I realized it must be nearly dinnertime. "Let's go eat, I'm starving. Come with us, Jeannie?"

"Sure, I'd like that, if you don't mind me butting in." She looked at Margaret.

"You're not butting in, Jeannie. We'd love to have you." I had to smile at the way Margaret had made Jeannie our guest. We were becoming a couple, I guess.

I paid the cleaning woman and got her phone number for later. We left without locking the doors because there weren't any locks, they'd been smashed. Add a locksmith to the list.

The short man preceded us, the tall man followed, and we walked the two blocks to a cafe that looked, if anything, worse than my apartment. But the tables and the silverware were clean and the food was delicious. Margaret enjoyed her sausage, finishing her gravy with great swipes of Italian bread.

I tried to keep the conversation general, no "Remember this" or "Remember that" with Jeannie. I didn't want Margaret to feel left out. We had only known each other for a few days, hardly long enough for us to have anything to remember. Except for the swamp and bed. I remembered everything about bed, but I didn't consider bed to be dinner conversation.

Margaret and I ordered iced tea, and I was happy to see that Jeannie did too. I wondered about her drinking. Jeannie and I had shared first love, had made what we believed to be permanent commitments. She did leave me, but I bear some of the fault.

"How's Freddie?" I asked. Not that I really cared.

Jeannie had been happy with me before Freddie entered the picture. Freddie had a yacht with a full bar, and Jeannie began to need a full bar, our meager resources unable to furnish booze in the amounts Jeannie soon consumed. She'd swim the short distance out to Freddie's boat, they'd spend the evening drinking, then Freddie would row Jeannie home. Jeannie always soused to the gills, smelling of booze and sex.

"Freddie's fine. She's with some real estate people

until this evening. We're going to open a lesbian bar and restaurant."

"A bar," Margaret said. "Where?"

"Here in New Orleans if we can find a place. Freddie's tired of the high seas, wants to settle on dry land for a while." Jeannie looked at me. "I stopped drinking a year ago. Haven't touched a drop in all that time." *Please believe me, please be happy for me, please love me again,* her eyes said.

I choked, tea dribbling down my front. "Ah, that's great. I'm glad to hear it." Surely I was mistaken. I had wanted her sober, wanted her love, but that was years ago. I was completely over wanting her, right?

"A bar sounds like fun." Margaret leaned towards Jeannie. "If you drank wouldn't it be dangerous to run a bar with liquor so available? Too much temptation?"

"No," Jeannie said quietly, looking at me. "I'm over that now. I don't have that problem anymore."

Our guards had taken the table nearest the door, and I saw that they had finished eating also, so I called for our check. "My treat," I said when Jeannie reached across the table for it.

I didn't want to hear her say that she was over Freddie, too, but I felt it coming. They were here together, but that didn't say much. Jeannie and I had been together in Florida, and I knew how little that had meant.

"Freddie and I'd like to hear about your adventure," Jeannie said to Margaret as we walked back to Esplanade. "Would you like to have breakfast with us tomorrow, or lunch?"

Margaret put her arm through mine, I liked the firmness of her touch. "It's up to Sarah. I'm game."

She tightened her hold. In front of the world, she was holding my arm. She looked at me, her eyebrows raised in question.

I started to object. We had too much of everything to do, and it was awkward having those men dogging our every step. Besides, I didn't have my car. It was still at Lonnie's place. Plus we had to do something about the Beauvoir. Margaret needed clothes, she also needed to meet with the district attorney, and she should probably see a doctor at least one more time. On and on.

I realized that none of these things would suffer if we spent an hour or so over a meal with Jeannie and Freddie. I just didn't want to do it. And I didn't want to explain to Margaret why not. Jeannie's presence was bothersome.

I took a deep breath and squeezed Margaret's arm. "We'd have to come from across the lake, so lunch would be better, we wouldn't have to rush." We'd reached my place. Our guards waited patiently while we talked. "Tell you what, give me your number and we'll call later to set a time."

"Jeannie seems to be a nice person, and I wouldn't mind meeting Freddie. To tell the truth, I feel like I'm in jail at your father's place. I liked being out today, meeting your friend." She laughed, "After lunch tomorrow I'll know three lesbians, won't I?"

Ha! She had picked up on Jeannie right away. To me, Jeannie was, if anything, more beautiful than I remembered. I had liked Jeannie naked, of course, also in beach clothes, or a swimsuit, but I had an instant sexual turn on when Jeannie wore hose and heels and a skirt. There was something about her slim ankles, and the hose clinging to her legs, the smoothness of silk between her soft thighs, the skirt an invitation, unrestricting, open.

She liked to stand with her legs slightly apart, inviting me to reach under the skirt, to touch the wetness I'd find.

Margaret was talking. I had to shift gears to get my mind off Jeannie and sex. "I'm glad she has her Freddie," Margaret was saying. "She's an attractive woman. I'd be jealous." I let that pass.

"Tell you what," I said as we were getting out of the car. "Let's go for a swim. I can lend you one of my suits."

"Are you talking about a swim in the pool, or a swim in that lake?"

"Either," I answered. "Or both."

"I think I'd prefer the pool, if it's the same to you. The lake is probably full of crocodiles."

I laughed my way up the stairs. "Alligators, Margaret, there aren't any crocodiles in Louisiana."

Trying on my suit led to other things. We didn't swim. Margaret was delighted at my enthusiasm. "If this is what happens when I try on clothes," she warned, "we'd better take a blanket when we go shopping. I have a feeling we'll end up on the fitting room floor."

I hushed her with a kiss, and snuggled her head under my chin. I didn't want her to see the shame in my eyes. I hadn't been making love with her. No.

I had been fucking Jeannie. My fantasy had taken me back to the tiny boathouse we'd shared, the single bed, Jeannie open, wet, waiting.

As I calmed my breathing, I thought, Vinnie Scalio was trying to kill us. I was trying to solidify a relationship with Margaret, my balloon was draped over the Manchac Swamp, my business needed attention, my apartment and office needed total overhauls. I didn't need another problem.

CHAPTER 15

"I'm having your car brought here this afternoon,
Lonnie told me. He'd been called on an emergency. A
Liberian freighter was in trouble at the Mississippi
River pass. It would be days before we'd see him
again. My father was cutting into his steak, Martha
hovering behind him.

"Does that mean I can drive without an escort? I
like not being shot at, but I like to do my own
driving, too." I winked at Margaret. She was every
bit as tired as I was of the constant attention. Our
"guards" didn't say much, didn't do much that I

could see except for driving and watching front, back and sideways. I'm surprised they didn't follow us to the bathroom.

"Yes, Sarah, you are now free to do your thing." I had to laugh at father's attempt to be hip. It was part of the reason I loved him.

"Do you think Vinnie Scalio has given up on Margaret and me?" I fervently hoped so. The tape, that incriminating audio/visual document, had been copied ad-nauseam and was now in the many hands of authority, ready to help nail Scalio to the wall.

Margaret was to give her deposition next Monday; mine was to follow. I couldn't see that anything I had to say would either help or hinder, but I was called on to give it and I knew the procedure.

"Your troubles are over, Sarah. You and Mrs. Paige are now free to do your things." He did like to repeat what sounded good to him. In the courtroom he was not given to witticisms or slang, thank goodness. Only at home, and that mostly to Martha who was always nearby.

"Do you know something we don't?" I asked him. Scalio was still free, sought but not found. I looked at Margaret and wiggled my eyebrows, now that we're free, watch out!

"Sarah, accept what I tell you." He took a bite of steak. "I have enjoyed having you here, but I will also enjoy it when you are settled back in town." That's my father plain-speaking. He never tries to varnish the truth. "This has nothing to do with you, Mrs. Paige."

What he said went in one ear, and out the other. I knew how worried he had been since that night at the motel. I rose from the table, kissed the top of his head. "Does that mean we're free this minute?"

He looked at his watch. "Yes, I believe so," he smiled.

My car had been polished, was full of gas, the door pockets emptied of candy wrappers and gasoline charge tickets.

"Where would you like to go?" I asked Margaret.

"How about a tour of the countryside?" Margaret settled herself next to me, her hand on my thigh.

I could look at her now, only slightly uncomfortable over the sexual fantasy which I had played out on her smooth body. The further away in time, the less guilty I felt. Margaret was wearing my blouse and a pair of my slacks, her legs crossed, no hose or skirt to invite exploration. I thought about how she'd looked that first day. She had been wearing hose, heels and a skirt. I think that's why I was attracted to her. Now, of course, it was her innocence in bed, her eagerness, and her wide-eyed honesty.

Time now to talk about a future, a future together. "Margaret," I started, "we have to talk."

"About us, of course. I wondered how long it would take for you to introduce the subject. You want to know what we're going to do, don't you? How we're going to handle our attraction for each other. And what about Ralph, the distance between New Orleans and Boston, your business, my job . . ."

"Whoa! One thing at a time."

"Okay, what first?"

"Ralph."

"No, I don't think that's first. For myself, I need to explore our physical feelings for each other. Since we first made love, I haven't been able to think about anything but you, your body, the way you touch me, arouse me. I have never felt that way before, Sarah. I could excite myself right now just thinking of your hands on me, your mouth on mine." She shifted uneasily. "I have to ask if this is going to last. Do lesbians keep this up?"

I had to concentrate to keep the car on the road. She wondered if lesbian sexual love lasts. I didn't have an answer for her. I loved her, but I had already been unfaithful in my thoughts, just as Jeannie had been unfaithful to me in deed. Freddie took sex from anybody who'd open their legs, and I had been screwing around regularly. How could I answer her question? I cleared my throat.

"Margaret, I don't know how long, or even if our kind of love lasts. I think it does. I know couples who have been together for years, but I don't know if they go at it like we're doing now. Frankly, I doubt it, but isn't it the same way with straight couples?"

She pressed my thigh. "Of course it is. There are as many ways of being a couple as there are people. Ralph and I are together for convenience. He's gay. I know now that I am, too. We cover for each other because being together makes us both respectable." Her hand moved higher up my leg. "I think, as far as the sex is concerned, that I'm satisfied with us, with us the way we are. I'll take what we have now, and if it changes later, I'll manage that, too."

"Okay, but what about Ralph, and your job, and Boston?"

"It occurs to me —" her hand moved higher. "— that New Orleans would be a nice place to live. I haven't seen much of it, but I like boudin, maybe that's a starting place."

"Ralph?" I asked. "Your job?" I took my right hand from the wheel and placed it over Margaret's hand.

"Ralph won't be a problem. He told me before he left here that he liked you, that it was okay if I loved you. We're friends." I heard her sigh and I tightened my hand on hers. "My job is another thing altogether. I've worked hard to get as far as I have. The money is good, I like what I'm doing . . ."

"There're lawyers in Louisiana, Margaret, and my father can help. He likes you. I know he'd be happy to put out a word or two. We can count on that."

"But what's he going to think if I move down here, move in with you? He knows you're a lesbian, right?"

"Well, no, not exactly. That is, we haven't ever talked about it. Lonnie knows, of course, and Mabel." I was silent for several minutes.

She moved her hand, turned in the seat to face me. "Maybe you're not so sure this is what you want, Sarah. I know you want me physically, as I want you, but do you want to live with me?" She shook her head slowly. "Perhaps we shouldn't make a legal contract out of something so subjective. It takes the fun out of the chase, doesn't it?" She smiled a little woeful smile. "You see, I've been thinking this out for days — since we made love in the motel, as a matter of fact. I've been waiting for you to say something because I was afraid to broach the subject, afraid that what I wanted wasn't what you wanted."

"Since I held you that night, all I've wanted is to be with you. And I was afraid you wouldn't commit yourself because of Ralph, and your job. I'm not so wonderful that you'd change your whole life to be with me . . ."

She hushed me, her fingers gentle on my lips. "I think you are more than wonderful, Sarah."

Too much. It was all too much. Falling in love with Margaret, then having Jeannie available — all this was too much. Tears began to stream down my cheeks. I couldn't see the road.

"Please don't cry." Margaret wiped my tears with a tissue and began crying too.

"I don't know why I'm crying," I said between sniffles, "I don't know why." But I did. I knew why.

We met Freddie and Jeannie at their downtown hotel. I had never seen very much of Freddie in the daylight. It was always late evening when she'd beach her rowboat and half-carry Jeannie to our door. She wouldn't say anything, either, just transfer Jeannie from her arms to mine, then stalk back to her boat. I once asked her why she didn't just keep Jeannie for the night. Her reply was a short laugh and a shrug, the meaning of both obscure.

Jeannie was always so hung over it would have been a waste of time asking her anything. One night Freddie simply didn't bring her back. The end.

We filled our plates at the extravagant buffet, sat knee to knee in a semicircular booth, paid close attention to the food and didn't talk. Jeannie's eyes were swollen and red. Freddie was huffy with silent fury. Margaret and I played our napkin game, none of which was lost on Freddie. Jeannie avoided my eyes. I had the distinct feeling that Freddie wasn't happy about having lunch with Margaret and me.

In for a penny, in for a pound. I asked, "Did you find the property you wanted, Freddie?"

Her head jerked up. "Huh?" she said gruffly.

"The property," I repeated. "The property you were looking for yesterday."

She looked puzzled for a second, then said, "I wasn't looking for property yesterday."

Whoops! I opened my mouth, but nothing came out. Margaret poked my thigh, put the napkin next to her plate. "Come with me to get a refill, Sarah." She stood and smiled around the table. "Bring back anything for anyone?"

I put my napkin on the table, too. I said, "If the waiter comes by, get me more tea, will you?" I said this to Jeannie, ashamed for her, sorry that her eyes had filled with tears. I wished I was a million miles away.

Back at the buffet, I stood close to Margaret. "I don't even want to know what's going on," she said quietly. "Finish your food. Let's get out of here."

I put some fruit in a tiny bowl, handed it to Margaret, then filled another bowl for myself. Slowly, we made our way back to our booth. Freddie was gone. Jeannie's tears were flowing freely.

"I'm sorry," she said, dabbing at her eyes with the napkin. "I didn't want it to be like this. I . . . we aren't getting along. I don't know where she was yesterday. And . . . and I don't have any place to go."

Was Freddie leaving Jeannie on my doorstep again? It hurt me to see Jeannie like this, no more than flotsam for Freddie to wash away like mud on the deck. I stood, my heart sorrowing for Jeannie, afraid for Margaret and me.

Margaret sat down and put her arm around Jeannie's shoulder, then looked up. "Can we help?" she questioned me.

I didn't answer. Help with what, I asked myself. We could give her money, certainly, but she needed more than that. Both of them were looking at me, Jeannie's face frightened, Margaret frowning at the injustice. Freddie had not made a very good impression.

Our waiter handed the check to me. This brought fresh tears. People were looking our way. Jeannie handed me a room key. "Use this," she said. "Freddie has plenty."

Margaret took the key from my hand, gave it back to Jeannie, then took Jeannie's arm. "We're going to the dressing room, Sarah. We'll meet you in the lobby."

After a while I saw them cross the carpeted expanse toward me. Jeannie's face was serene, no tears, her hair in place, chin up, her Venus-like body causing heads to turn.

Clearly, she was being escorted by Margaret. More heads turned. Their arms entwined, in step, they advanced, and my knees turned to jelly. I had made love to both, had whispered "I love you" to both.

"Wake up, Sarah," Margaret hissed. I guess I'd gone into a trance, my thoughts scattering. "We're going upstairs." They turned and headed for the elevators.

Margaret, apparently, had taken charge. She held out her hand for the room key, opened the door and entered first. Freddie was gone, nothing of hers remained in the room.

Jeannie darted to the closet, sighing with relief when she saw the few things hanging there. "Well, at least she left me something to wear."

There was a small overnight case on the rack at the foot of the bed. "Pack." Margaret's tone was steely, reminding me of last Friday, and how she sounded at the prison. Jeannie seemed relieved to have someone tell her what to do. Freddie had trained her well.

With Margaret's help, the few things from the closet, and toiletries from the bathroom, were soon zipped out of sight. Margaret called the desk. Freddie had checked out, paying the bill in full.

The three of us walked to the garage. "Where to, ladies?" I asked when my car appeared.

"Shopping," said Margaret. "I don't have a thing to wear."

CHAPTER 16

Much later, as I parked at my father's, I said to Margaret, "I need to talk with Jeannie. Do you mind?"

She shook her head. "No." Her generous smile was directed at Jeannie, her blue eyes understanding. "Just help me upstairs with these packages, then you two can talk down here where it's private."

After we helped Margaret, I ushered Jeannie into my father's study. I sat facing her across the desk. "You know what we have to talk about, don't you?" I began. "I want to know why you left, what prompted you to disappear like that, and why you think you'd be welcome now, after all this time." If my questions sounded clinical, too bad.

She tossed her head, some of her old spirit returning now that we were alone. "Is that important? Really, it's been so long."

"Yes, it's important." I needed to know what aberration of mine had caused Jeannie to leave. Knowing might keep me from future failure. I wouldn't make the same mistake with Margaret if I knew what I had done wrong with Jeannie.

"There wasn't any money," she said bluntly, "and you were boring, always wanting to work, work, work! We stopped having fun, you didn't like my friends —"

"Jeannie," I interrupted. "We had to work. We had a business."

"Phooey, it wasn't worth piss, and you know it." Her voice was cold, flat.

"But it could have been worth something, if I'd had some help," I protested.

"So it's my fault?"

"I didn't say that. If we'd worked together, like we planned, we could have been successful. Our classes were getting bigger. Some money was coming in; we had a good thing going."

"Good for you, maybe, you could always fall back on your father's money. What did I have?"

I cringed at the bitterness in her tone. Had our love fallen apart over money? I remember resisting the temptation to call my father when we were short of cash. I also remember frequent arguments, not about money exactly, but usually brought on by the lack thereof.

"I don't recall that we missed any meals," I said lamely.

"Sarah, I got tired of beans and wieners. I got tired of staying in that dilapidated old shack, of you always on me about something. And that's another thing — you thought having sex day and night was a substitute for no money, no friends —"

"I didn't think that, Jeannie, I thought you wanted to make love as much as I did. At least we had that going for us, even if we didn't have a lot else."

Jeannie's face was sullen. She avoided my eyes. "Maybe we did, at first. But even that got boring."

I gulped, remembering the wildness of our lovemaking, how Jeannie would cling, crying for more. I pictured her on our tiny bed, thrashing and moaning, sobbing for me to go faster, deeper, harder... *Now,* she'd scream, *now, give it to me now!* After her climax, I'd lie there sweating, my heart racing, physically exhausted. I thought we were making love. We weren't at all. I was simply providing a service, I saw now.

There *had* been a certain sameness to our sexual activities. Whichever of us initiated it, Jeannie would fondle me until, aroused, I would come in a rush. Then it was her turn, and I did everything she asked. I was in love. When didn't I do what she wanted?

"What did Freddie do in bed that I didn't?"

Jeannie blushed. "Sarah, I didn't mean that. Our lovemaking didn't get boring, but Freddie had money. One night I asked her to take me away, and she did." Jeannie closed her eyes. "She was awful in bed.

144

Honest, she wanted me to do everything, and she hardly ever made me come. I had to do that for myself. With her watching, of course." Jeannie's bluntness certainly painted a picture for me, vivid, graphic.

"Why did you come to New Orleans?" I asked, not wanting to hear any more about Freddie's sexual practices.

"Freddie really did talk about opening a bar and restaurant here. She didn't need the money, but she thought it would be a good way to meet gay people. I didn't think it was such a great idea, but I liked the thought of seeing you." There was a long pause. "I think she got really tired of me when I stopped drinking. When I was sober, I wouldn't perform naked for her friends, I wouldn't let everyone on board have me."

"Have you?" I am not so naive that I didn't know what she meant. The question just popped out.

"Freddie likes to watch other people have sex. She especially likes to watch me with a man." Jeannie's face flushed. She stared over my head. "Freddie wouldn't let a man touch her, but she liked to watch them touch me, among other things."

"I don't believe this! Why did you stay?" The Jeannie I loved wouldn't have been a party to such debauchery. She would have thumbed her nose at Freddie's perversions, wouldn't she?

"What else could I do?" Jeannie's expression changed. "It wasn't all that terrible, not when I was drunk. I don't know why I stopped boozing. I think I got sick of a constant hangover, and I just quit all at once. And when I stopped being Freddie's prize exhibit, she was ready to trade me in. We've been fighting like animals for months, and short of jumping overboard, what options do I have?"

I could answer her honestly. Tell her that, except for the added years, she seemed to be the same beautiful, sexy, selfish, untrained, unambitious, immature person she had always been. Maybe she could start from there.

I clasped my hands, stared at my lap, cleared my throat. "What do you want me to say? That I'm not angry anymore? That I still want you?" I shook my head. "Well, I don't want you. I'm not angry. I got over that a long time ago, but I also got over wanting you." Except, I thought, for that one little lapse the other night.

Jeannie looked stricken. Tears filled her eyes. She covered her face and began sobbing.

"Crying won't change anything, Jeannie. There's nothing for you here."

"What am I going to do? I don't have any money, no place to go . . . please, Sarah, help me, please. You have so much." Her sobs were genuine, and I could tell she was afraid.

Yes, I did have a lot. I had a loving family, a kind and caring woman waiting upstairs and a business of my own. As a young, healthy lesbian, what more could I ask?

"Jeannie," I began slowly, not knowing what I was going to say, but gaining inspiration as I spoke. "I'll give you enough money to hold you for a while. I suggest you get your ass back to the Keys, get a job and take charge of your life." I'm not schoolmarmish by nature, but I understood Jeannie. My voice harsh, I added, "I don't owe you anything,

146

understand, so there won't be a repeat. You can stay here tonight, then tomorrow Margaret and I will take you to the bus, or whatever, and that's the end as far as I'm concerned."

Now that salvation was at hand, her look became sly, furtive. "Does Margaret know about us?" she asked.

"I haven't told her, no. And there isn't any 'us' to tell her. We're ancient history, believe me." I knew what was coming.

"Well, maybe she'd like to know." Now Jeannie's look was appraising, calculating.

"Maybe she would," I said. I buzzed the large bedroom upstairs. "Margaret, will you come to the study, please." I sat, waited, watching Jeannie's expression change.

Margaret was still dressed in my clothes, her expression curious but serene. "What, Sarah?"

"Jeannie has something to tell you."

Margaret pulled a chair to the desk and faced Jeannie. "Yes?"

Jeannie had apparently decided to brave it out. "Sarah and I were lovers once, and we still could be."

Margaret smiled slowly. "I know that," she said to Jeannie. "But I don't believe Sarah wants you anymore. Do you, Sarah?"

I think my mouth had dropped open, but I recovered. "No" was all I could say.

"Well, if that's all, I'd like to finish hanging up my clothes." She smiled at Jeannie, smiled at me, and left the room.

* * * * *

147

"This is the first time I've worn a nightgown for you." Margaret showed me front, back, and both sides. "Do you like it?"

My father taught an evening extension class in Slidell, and supper, which was late, had been a quiet affair. He was going over class notes, and acknowledged Jeannie's greeting with a smile and a nod, then didn't say another word as he ate and made careful notations on each page.

Margaret and I carried on a subdued conversation, mostly about the clothes Margaret had bought earlier, the mess in my apartment and office, and the feasibility of hiring a contractor rather than trying to coordinate the work myself. When my father excused himself immediately after coffee, Jeannie stalked to the upstairs room which Martha had prepared for her. Margaret and I watched TV in the study, then climbed the stairs hand in hand.

"I like the gown," I answered. "It's a shame you won't get to sleep in it."

Margaret raised the hem. "Help me?" she asked.

I was sitting on the edge of the bed, already undressed, and I pulled Margaret to me. Sliding my hands under the silken hem, I raised the gown by touching every inch of her I could reach. "You are so warm," I breathed, "and so soft." I pulled the gown over her head and embraced her. "You have depths, my love. How did you know about Jeannie?"

"Clear as the nose on your face." Gently, she urged me to lie down on my back. She cradled my head, offering a breast for my mouth to take. I took, my hand taking the other. "Your Jeannie is transparent. When she walked into your apartment earlier, I knew. You turned bright red and did everything possible to keep away from her."

As I squeezed and sucked, Margaret cupped her breast, offering more. She began kissing my head. I doubled my efforts, now inviting her to lie atop me, so that both breasts were available to my mouth.

"You were so funny," Margaret whispered. "You wouldn't look at me or at Jeannie and especially not at Freddie. Yours was a guilty conscience if I've ever seen one. And I've seen plenty." Margaret's breathing had quickened, we shifted positions so that our faces were touching. We kissed. Now my breathing was almost out of control too. We kissed some more.

"I didn't tell you because Jeannie was so long ago. She doesn't have the same place in my life."

I ran my tongue over her body, leaving slippery trails, making her jerk abruptly as I licked a sensitive spot. I straddled her resting my haunches on her hips, and she reached for my breasts, a touch like feathers. As I began to move, grinding my wetness into her soft pubic hair, her touch became firmer, her nails like talons raking my flesh. Spasms of pure delight spiraled through my body.

I looked down at her closed eyes, her face a picture of pleasure, and I bent to kiss her mouth again, tenderly. She looked at me, her hands still stroking my breasts, and her smile showed love like I had never seen.

"Let me do this," she said. I nodded, and we changed positions. She rocked over me, her hips moving slowly. I heard soft groans of pleasure as she rubbed against me, felt her moisture, the heat as she moved faster and her summit neared.

The roaring in my ears was so loud I couldn't think. Instinct drove me. I moved her to my side, opened her legs, took her wetness in my mouth and brought her to a shuddering climax. For a long time she lay quiet in my arms.

"We've never made love the same way twice, have we?"

"I don't think so," I whispered in her ear.

"When we get to the end, can we start again?"

"I think so, if we're not too old."

"What I really enjoy is the lesson. You teach me how it's done, then I practice, right?"

"Right," I said.

"I'm ready to practice, Sarah."

"And I'm ready, too. Will you tell me something first?"

"You want to know why I wasn't bothered about Jeannie, don't you? Why I wasn't jealous." Her voice was a soft murmur.

"You continually surprise me. I don't know of one person who wouldn't be, well . . . slightly angry about Jeannie. You know she was trying to threaten me, don't you? I had promised to stake her. She was trying for more, I think."

"Of course she was. But, Sarah, I do feel sorry for her. Living with Freddie must have been horrible."

"You don't know the half of it, and you don't want to know. Jeannie hasn't grown up. She's still the person she was years ago. I don't know why I loved her."

"It probably had something to do with sex, don't you think?"

"I guess so. Anyway, we're driving her to the bus tomorrow, and I hope we've heard the last of her."

"Sarah," Margaret said patiently, "I'm ready to practice."

"Margaret," I said, "your teacher is ready."

CHAPTER 17

At breakfast, I asked Jeannie if she had any idea about her travel schedule, figuring that she probably hadn't made any effort to find out what was available. When she shook her head, I told her, "Margaret and I have to get into town right after eating, and I'll drive you in with us, to wherever you need to go, bus or train, but I'm not going to come back here for you. Unless you want to walk across the lake, better get ready now."

Jeannie threw her napkin on the table, and

stomped upstairs. I shrugged, grinning. Margaret frowned at me.

"Be kind," she cautioned, "she's all alone."

I called for bus, train and, as an afterthought, plane schedules, figuring that Jeannie wouldn't think twice about blowing a good chunk of whatever I gave her on a plane to Key West. I was right. She chose the ten o'clock direct flight to Miami, leaving open the trip from Miami to the Keys. How she chose to travel those last miles wasn't up to me. I made her reservation, then shooed both of them to the car.

At the bank I gave Jeannie five hundred over the cost of her ticket, which bottomed out my account. She sniffed with disdain at the meagerness of the amount. I had to snort when she asked, "What interest are you charging me, Shylock?" She was probably trying to impress Margaret, because she and I both knew I'd never see a dime of the money.

I did seventy over the causeway, but we reached the airport in time for Jeannie to pick up her ticket.

"Don't call me," she said. "And I won't call you." Then she yanked her suitcase off the seat, slammed the door, and disappeared through the glass doors of the terminal.

"That's a good idea, Sarah. Don't call her."

"Margaret, I have no intention of ever seeing her again. She's ancient history, believe me."

I took Airline Highway to town because Margaret wanted to see the city, and the interstate isn't great for sightseeing. On the way, we continued discussing the pros and cons of hiring a contractor to do the makeover of my office and the apartment.

As we crossed Tulane Avenue, I remembered that

Mabel had said she'd go to the office to meet the telephone installer, so I headed for Magazine Street. I wanted to talk with her about hiring a contractor, and I'd already decided to look for one who would promise renovations done fast. Mabel knew everybody in Orleans Parish. She'd know a name.

Mabel was sitting in a lawn chair she'd brought from home. It was the only whole piece of furniture in the room. She reached for Margaret's hand. "Are you feeling better, dear?"

She didn't need to ask, really. Margaret wore slacks and a blouse that she'd bought yesterday, and she positively glowed. I couldn't look anywhere but at her.

Still holding Margaret's hand, Mabel said, "I've been thinking about this place and your apartment, and the only thing that comes to mind is a contractor to coordinate all the work that has to be done on both." She looked at me. "It's time for you to make some decisions, Sarah."

"That's what we were discussing on the way here, but I don't know a contractor to call, do you? I don't think it's a good idea just to pick a number out of the phone book. We have to hire someone we can work with, who won't balk at making changes halfway through." Margaret was grinning. "Not that I change my mind that much," I said, grinning back at her.

Mabel grunted, shaking her head. "Of course you don't," she said, adding, "I've heard of two women contractors who do excellent work, so I've been told. Shall I call?"

I looked at Margaret. She raised her eyebrows in that way she has of asking a question and answering it at the same time. Now we were both grinning like silly teenagers. Mabel looked at us and nodded, her open smile causing wrinkles around her brown eyes.

"We'll see how soon they can get started," she said.

"I thought your niece was going to help you today." I was navigating Magazine Street, trying not to hit the pedestrians who dashed from between parked cars, and the cars that pulled into traffic right in front of me without warning of any kind.

"She's at your apartment now. We hired a truck to take all that loose stuff to the dump, get the floors cleared so you could see what you wanted done. I think the most insulting thing is the spray paint on the walls. They had already torn the apartment to pieces. Why add insult to injury?"

"Because," Margaret said, "that's just what they wanted to do. Add insult. I wonder if the police have made any headway?" Margaret was sandwiched on the front seat between Mabel and me, her hand on my thigh. Mabel couldn't help but see.

"The insurance agent who was checking the claim for your apartment and office this morning said Scalio's still missing. The young man seemed to know who had done the damage, and why. He asked about Ragtime. Is there some reason you haven't filed that claim, Sarah?"

"No," I answered. "I asked Dad to call the insurance company for me, but I didn't mention Ragtime. I guess I thought we'd have to drag her out of the swamp to find out how much damage had been done. That means renting a helicopter . . ." I had a sudden vision of Ragtime, with more holes than a colander, draped at the end of a metal line, swinging helplessly over the swamp. "I have time to take care of that," I added. Margaret patted my thigh.

For maybe the second time in history, I parked directly in front of my house. A cloud of dust was billowing out the bedroom doors, and we watched Mabel's niece sweeping chunks of tile and Sheetrock into a truck backed up to the balcony. Someone had had the presence of mind to take down a section of the corn-cob fence that protected my tiny patio from the street and to unbolt a portion of the balcony's iron rail so that debris could be shoveled or swept right into the truck bed.

The apartment was empty of furniture; it was totally bare.

"The insurance agent took pictures of your stuff, then said we could haul it away. This mess —" the niece pointed with her broom. — "is all that's left. We've made four trips to the dump already. This should be the last." Her voice sounded hollow in the empty rooms. She turned to attack the pile of scraps, sweeping briskly toward the balcony.

Taking a deep breath, I said, "If I could move right now into a nice, new condo, I would. I'd walk out of this and never look back. I simply couldn't afford to. The rent from two apartments on the second floor took care of the note for this place so I could live rent free. The insurance will cover some of this, but I'm still going to have to come up with a wad. I don't even have a business anymore." I felt my eyes fill with tears. I was feeling sorry for myself, the proverbial bystander caught up in a hurricane of woe.

"Sarah, we don't love you for your money. We love you because you're you." Mabel moved closer, her expression anxious. "You know I'll give you whatever you need. If you won't let me help, call on your father." She turned to Margaret. "This child came back from Florida flat broke. She's built a business, bought this house, a car, a truck and her balloon, by working harder than anyone I've known. She wouldn't take anything from her father, or from me, either. I think it's time she let us help, don't you?"

Margaret was nodding. "Yes," she said softly. "I think so, too."

My father was in the study talking to a tall man. They were looking at some papers spread out on the desk. I gave a little wave as Margaret and I passed by.

"Sarah," my father called. "Come in here for a minute, please. You, too, Mrs. Paige."

The man straightened. "I'm Sheriff Morrison, little lady." He took my hand in his huge paw, saying, "We've found your recording stuff, ma'am, all piled in a warehouse on the west bank. The identifying numbers match, and everything seems to be okay."

My knees almost gave way. Getting my equipment back would save a couple of thousand dollars that I didn't have. It meant that I was back in business! I looked up at the grizzled face. "All of it?" I asked.

"Everything you listed. There's enough stuff in

that building to start a small city." He looked at my father, who nodded slightly. "And we'll bring it here to you in a couple of days."

"How did he know which of us was you?" Margaret whispered as we made our way upstairs.

"I don't know. Maybe he saw the picture of me on Dad's shelf." I was bounding up the stairs, pulling Margaret behind me. "We have serious talking to do, ma'am," I said. "We've gotta get some things straight."

"Right now I want to know why Scalio was warehousing the things he didn't have destroyed on the spot. It seems dumb to keep the evidence against him in a place that could be found, don't you think?"

"Probably wasn't his idea." I opened the door to my room. "His goons maybe stashed things to sell someday. Maybe Scalio didn't know anything about it. Anyway, who knows what people do?"

"I know what you do," Margaret said, as I turned the lock behind us. "You do nice things to me."

"Yes, but this time I want to talk before I do those nice things." I pulled the rocking chair to the bed, sat Margaret in it, and made myself comfortable against the headboard.

Before I could speak, Margaret held up her hand, palm facing me. "I have some things to say, too. Since I'm the guest here, I'll go first."

I thought, now she was going to tell me why we couldn't be together, why she had to go back to Boston.

"I have a dozen commitments in Boston," she began. "I'm not a person to let things drift, nor do I abandon my responsibilities. I have to take care of things, make a clean break, before I can even consider moving here to live with you."

We hadn't really talked at any length about the possibility of her staying here with me, or of our living together. She must have known that was what I wanted.

"But you are considering it?"

She smiled at me. A gentle, loving smile. "I'm not impulsive, either. When I picked you to take Rancatore's deposition, I was acting out of need. The other videographers were highly recommended, too. I picked you because you're a lesbian, and I needed a lesbian."

"You wanted to play with me, didn't you?" I had a picture of her kneeling to help me pick up the spilled contents of my purse that day in the House of Detention. I remembered the depths in her blue eyes as she put the chocolate mints in my hand.

"Yes, Sarah, I wanted to play with you." Margaret leaned forward. I leaned also. We kissed. Somehow, we didn't get around to restarting the conversation that day.

On Monday, each of us gave our deposition. Because of a cancellation the contractors were able to begin sooner than we'd thought. On Wednesday of that week we watched as the apartment began to look like new under the capable hands of a crew of lesbian carpenters, plasterers, and painters.

Over coffee that afternoon I said to her, "Margaret, I don't want you to do something irrevocable that you'll regret. We can stop this, you know." Although I knew that I couldn't stop anything, I wanted her to have the freedom to do what she felt necessary. It hadn't been two weeks since we had met. Could we base a lifetime on two weeks?

The news came on Thursday of that week. Scalio's body had washed up on the Mississippi levee in the surge from a passing freighter. There was not much cause for rejoicing, but we weren't sad, either.

That evening she said, "I'm leaving on the fifteenth. Will you drive me to the airport?"

She had been in touch with her office, and with Ralph, almost every day, so I had known the dreaded time was near. I just hadn't figured it would be so soon. We had settled nothing between us, made no decisions.

Hardly speaking, we sat together in the passenger terminal. When her plane was called, I took her hand in both of mine.

"Margaret," I said. "I love you. I want you to be with me, but I don't want you to ruin your life . . ." I couldn't go on.

We embraced, and as I turned away, Margaret handed me a folded piece of paper. Then she walked away from me, down the loading corridor to the plane.

My hands trembling, I unfolded the note.

My darling Sarah,

You are afraid that I am going to do something that I will regret later in order to be with you now. I have thought a great deal about the changes that would be necessary for us to be together. It all comes down to a matter of priorities and what we have to do to achieve those things that are most important.

I practice law. I do this to make a living. While I enjoy my work, it is a means to an end and the place where I practice is not important in itself.

My marriage was convenient for both Ralph and me, and it has been comfortable. It has always had a sort of temporariness about it . . . it is not a major obstacle.

I love you. I want to be with you . . . if you want me or for as long as you want me.

I do not require "commitments" or verbal contracts from you. Just let me love you. Let me give you whatever you are willing and able to receive of my love. If we can share love for this moment . . . or for a month . . . or for a year or a lifetime, I will take what is offered.

Whatever regrets a lifetime can hold, I can never regret love. Let us share our dreams. Please wait for me.

Margaret

CHAPTER 18

Of course, I couldn't wait to call her. Figuring that the flight was three hours, the ride from the airport maybe one hour, I had a four hour wait, more or less. I waited less. The phone rang twice, then I heard her lovely, soft voice.

"Margaret," I said.

"Yes, Sarah," she replied.

"How did you know?"

"Because I wanted it to be you."

I began blinking to hold back the tears. My voice

choked, I said, "I have your note in my hand. If there was a question . . . about my waiting, that is . . . then the answer is yes, I'll wait for you. I'll wait days, weeks, months or however long it takes. But you knew that already, didn't you?"

"Yes. I knew. But I'm glad to hear you say it anyway."

"Pretty sure of me, aren't you?" Still fighting tears, I tried to joke.

"Yes, I'm sure." Her voice was calm, sober. No answering levity.

I began sniffing. "When I watched you walk away from me, I was afraid . . . no, I was sure we were through. We hadn't settled anything because I didn't want to rush you into something you weren't ready for."

"Sarah, stop this instant! You have not rushed me into anything. I love you, I want you . . . for now and for always. I am not going to change my mind!" She said quietly, "Read my note again, darling. It tells you exactly how I feel."

"Have you, ah, said anything to Ralph?"

She laughed. "Not yet. I want to sit him down and start at the beginning. He's in the kitchen now, mixing a drink. We've just walked into the house, darling. My purse is still in my hand."

"Well, I couldn't wait to call."

"I know," she said. "I'm glad you couldn't wait."

"Are you going back to work tomorrow?"

"I'm going to the office. I don't know how much work I'll do. Tomorrow, I'm resigning, but I'll probably have to give them some time to find a replacement."

"Margaret, I'm going to be patient if it kills me. There's a lot to do here, you know, but I won't be too busy to miss you."

"My love, while you're thinking of me there's a good chance I'm thinking of you." Her voice hushed, she said, "Especially of you in bed."

"Me too," I said eloquently.

I thought the days would drag. Some of them did. When I had depositions to take, they filled time during the day, but evenings and nights were mostly long and lonely. I stayed across the lake with my father, my apartment being empty of furniture but still full of paint cans and plaster and sawdust.

The stolen video and audio equipment was delivered to my father's house intact. Everything in working order, even the extra cords were accounted for. Scalio's men had taken good care of the things they figured to sell.

"Now that we know Scalio is dead, we don't have to worry about his gang trying to kill me, do we?" I asked my father.

My father looked up, rattling his newspaper. "No, I don't believe so. Most of them have left town from what I hear and I can't imagine that you pose a threat to any of them."

"What have you done about Ragtime?" Margaret asked one evening. I was despondent; I could hear it in my own voice. I deliberately hadn't asked her how much longer I'd have to wait. I knew she was doing what she had to do, as fast as she could, and I'd promised to be patient — a promise I found harder and harder to keep.

"Lonnie is going after what's left of her this weekend." He had returned from the emergency job during the past week. "He doesn't want me along. He thinks I'll bawl all over the place, and he's probably right." And, suddenly, my promise crumbled. "Margaret, I need you here. When are you coming?"

"Oh, my darling, please . . . I'll be with you soon. The things I want to keep are already in storage, and I'm living out of boxes. It won't be long. I miss you too, you know."

I sighed. It was not my intention to rush her, even if I could. I knew with certainty that she was going to do a thorough job, everything taken care of the way it should be . . . no sloppy endings for Margaret. She would make a clean break from her old life, leaving no trailing ends. That was what I wanted, too.

"Well, the apartment is mostly furnished now. Everything but the kitchen appliances, that is. Honey, somewhere along the line we mismeasured. The stove, the sink, the dishwasher, the fridge, the microwave and the oven won't all fit in the space we have. Not and have room for storage, shelves and the little dining table, too."

"Oh, dear. What are you going to do?"

"While they're hauling Ragtime out of the swamp, I'm going back to the store and redesign our kitchen, I guess. That'll keep me from thinking about what's happening."

"More than anything, I want to be with you. We

should be doing these things together. I'm so sorry all this is on your shoulders alone."

Remembering Jeannie's total lack of responsibility, I laughed.

"Sarah, I'm sending you a check to cover Ragtime's expenses this weekend.

"No, you're not. I don't need your money." This was an out-and-out lie. I'd be in hock for the next century or two, in spite of the insurance settlement. Renting the helicopter wasn't cheap. Completely refurbishing my apartment wasn't cheap. The furniture wasn't cheap, either. Ragtime had had insurance to cover liabilities, but Ragtime herself was a total loss. It would be years before I could buy another.

"You do so need money! You haven't let me pay for anything. I can imagine the state of your finances. I didn't want to fuss with you about who paid for what until I got there but I see that waiting wasn't the thing to do."

"We don't have to discuss this at all, Margaret."

"Yes, we do." Her voice, usually soft and controlled, was beginning to rise. "I am going to pay my share, Sarah. And my share is exactly half, understand. More than that, all — and I mean all — of Ragtime's loss is my fault. I wanted you to take me up that day even after you had called it quits. If it hadn't been for me, you wouldn't have been in this mess. I'm responsible, and I'm going to pay for it, understand?" There was enough steel in her voice to build another Sears Tower.

I am a person who likes to pay her own way. I'm stubborn about it. Too stubborn, I've been told. Margaret was also stubborn, I saw that now.

"Okay," I said meekly. We could fight about it later.

"Well," she said, "I'm glad you see it my way. And Sarah, the check had better be used."

The check was for five thousand. I used what I needed for Ragtime's rescue. The balance went into the bank.

The apartment was finally finished after four long weeks. It was complete with new locks on the doors and new furnishings in every room. I could have moved in, but I wanted it new, unlived-in, for both of us. Except for another picture of my mother, there wasn't an item that had memories attached to it. Margaret had sent several large boxes which I stored for the time being in the empty apartment across the hall. We had bed linens, kitchen things, towels and toiletries — everything we'd selected together, even light bulbs. It was to be our honeymoon suite. Only Margaret was missing.

"Sarah, I have something to tell you." It was a Sunday morning, and I was feeling lower than I had ever felt. Ragtime, what was left of her, was in a broken, torn heap behind the airport tool shed.

There was something different in her voice, a tone I didn't recognize. I suddenly got scared. Was she going to tell me she'd changed her mind, I thought.

"First, I need to know if you're free this evening."

"Free?" I asked stupidly.

"Yes, will you be free around six?"

"Uh huh, I think so. But why?"

"Because that's when my plane lands, darling." Suppressed excitement, that's what I'd heard. "I'll be home at six, my love, and I'll try to take away some of the pain." I had told her about Ragtime, and I'd cried at the telling. Now she was coming home.

The plane was on time. We embraced, and she kissed me full on the mouth. I started to tell her we should be a little more circumspect in public, but she hushed me, saying, "I know prudence is called for, but I couldn't help myself. I'll behave from now on."

I handed her a set of keys for the apartment. She opened the door and pulled me inside. Our embrace didn't end for two days.

Sunday afternoon I'd asked Mabel to do what she could with our work schedule, so Wednesday morning as I fixed coffee, I plugged in the phone and called her.

"How is Margaret?" Mabel asked.

"She's fine, just fine. Do we have to do any work this week?"

"No, you have until next Monday. I managed to get the dates changed, so we're okay until then. But Sarah, our schedule will be over our heads if we don't clear these people."

"Yes, Mother," I said. "Let's plan to have dinner next week, the three of us."

"You're sure? Does Margaret know about this invitation?"

"It was her idea, but I heartily approve."

"In that case, I'd be delighted."

CHAPTER 19

Friday, at noon, Margaret sat up in bed. "Sarah, I think it's time we talked about Ragtime, don't you?"

"No. I can't have her repaired, too much damage. Can't buy another, too much money. Suppose we make love instead." I reached for her, to pull her down so that I could stroke the soft places that so enthralled me.

"I'm interested in making love, Sarah, but do let's talk about Ragtime after." Our interests coinciding, we made love.

* * * * *

"Where's that newspaper for balloonists you told me about? They have classifieds for new and used balloon sales, right?" We were sitting at our tiny kitchen table, sipping tea, eating tuna sandwiches and pickled okra.

"Sure, but why?"

"It's time we bought Ragtime Number Two, Sarah."

"I don't think so, Margaret."

"Well, if you don't want another balloon, then I'll simply buy one and you can fly it. Or maybe I can find someone else to be my pilot. There must be dozens of nice ladies who'd jump at the opportunity."

I couldn't think of dozens, but there were a few scattered around.

"Okay, you can look at the ads."

Margaret was thorough with this, too. She looked through the paper for a few minutes then handed it back to me.

"The ads for balloons are written in some alien tongue. I can't understand one word. Tell me what these abbreviations mean."

"They're really not hard to understand if you know anything about ballooning." I pointed. "These are a few of the major brands, and when the ad says 'annual' with a date, that tells you when the last inspection was held." Margaret was trying to follow along.

"What does it mean, 'four hundred and eighty five hours, zero since annual'? "

"That's the total hours flown but it hasn't been flown at all since the annual inspection." I looked at

170

her. "Actually, if you were buying one used, you'd look for not more than about a hundred hours."

"New ones are expensive, but used balloons are costly, too. Look at this, nineteen thousand, but it does have dual burners." She smiled proudly. "I figured that one for myself. Ragtime only had one burner, right?"

"The burner you ignited that got us up and away, right."

"Do we want two burners?" I considered her question for a moment, then nodded. "Yes, I think so." Our heads together, we read the ads. I was getting excited. Maybe I could swing one of the cheaper ones. I could get a second mortgage, couldn't I?

"Sarah, I think Ragtime was a good size for us, don't you?"

"Yep, we can easily handle an X-seven. Even if there's only my brother as the chase crew, the three of us can get her packed back in the truck without too much strain. She's heavy, but the Tommy Gate does the lifting." Here I was, talking as if we'd decided not only to buy a balloon, but what size we wanted.

"Did you buy Ragtime new?"

"No, Dad's friend wanted a larger one, so he sold Ragtime at a good price. She was almost new, anyway." I reached for Margaret's hand. "I don't believe a new one is within my reach but let's send for pictures of a few of these used ones and, if we see a design we like, we'll do some talking."

Margaret hugged me. "We're looking for an envelope with bright colors like Ragtime, right?"

"Uh huh." I was marking a couple of ads that

looked promising. "Let's write . . . no, let's call these numbers, okay?"

Margaret, looking very pleased, said, "You call, I'll clean up here."

The following week, Margaret had a job interview, and Mabel and I did seven depositions. The three of us had dinner on Wednesday evening in the French Quarter. My bank account was beginning to look better, but I was far from being flush.

On Friday Margaret was hired by the city's most prestigious law firm. Besides the usual perks, they were offering a substantial starting bonus.

"Your resume must have wowed them," I said, shuffling through the pictures we'd received. None of the envelopes matched Ragtime's design, but we were looking at extras — padded tank covers, heat tapes for the tanks, a full instrument package, low hours, the right size, new hoses, dual burners and, of course, drop lines. Not that I expected each and every thing to be available but it wouldn't hurt to start out looking for the things we needed.

A couple of weekends later, as we were wrapped around each other in bed, Margaret squeezed me.

"Sarah," she whispered, "now that we've selected our balloon, we have to seriously discuss finances."

I jerked awake. "There's nothing to discuss."

"No, I guess there isn't, not really. I'm buying

Ragtime Two, in spite of your interminable objections. Now, go to sleep."

"Margaret —" I began.

Her hand covered my mouth. I relaxed in her arms, grumbling softly into the night. She giggled, a most un-Margaret sound. "Hush, baby," she said. I hushed.

For our first flight together I decided, because of the wind direction, to take off from the little town of Northlake, where there was a huge schoolyard vacant at six AM on a Saturday morning.

Lonnie started the fan and, much to Margaret's delight, he asked her to help hold the mouth of the envelope open so that it could be cold-inflated. When the balloon was close to being full, I ignited the burners, gave some very long blasts, and Ragtime Two began to right itself. The morning sun captured the brilliance of her spiral colors, and she danced flirtatiously in the early breeze. I had taken her up already, before we decided she was the one we wanted, but Margaret hadn't been there to see her inflated.

"She's beautiful, Sarah!" Margaret was actually dancing around outside the basket, looking up as Ragtime Two filled, then began to lift. "Beautiful, beautiful, beautiful!"

I was in the basket as it righted itself, then Lonnie helped Margaret aboard. He was grinning like an idiot as he waved us off. Very adult-like, I stuck out my tongue.

Lonnie and I did a radio check, then I handed the radio to Margaret. "You press this button to talk to Lonnie. We'll be in almost constant contact with him. He has a map of the area like the one we have and we'll help him follow us on the ground so that he can find us when we land."

We were drifting west, but our flight would end before we reached the Manchac Swamp. Margaret was fascinated, leaning over the side watching people and houses, cars and cows, as we glided silently overhead, the crackle of the radio and the whoosh of flame our only sound.

Ten minutes into our flight, Margaret turned to me. "I know we can't make love, but do you think a little kiss would be okay? I'm so happy and excited, Sarah! I had no idea it would be like this."

"A kiss and a hug," I answered her. "The rest will wait until later."

I kept us at fifteen hundred feet, and we seemed to be standing still, the earth moving on a slow track beneath us. The winds were gentle and steady, our direction predictable. Several times we identified Lonnie as he switched from one road to another in order to follow as closely as possible.

Margaret had to point out everything she saw. Once she said, "If I ever wondered what happened to abandoned cars, I've found out. They're parked in the backyards."

I looked down. "Margaret, my love, we're flying over rural Louisiana. That's the way it's done here."

A little over an hour into our flight I began to look for landing sites. We were now flying over mostly empty fields separated by piney woods. I needed space that wasn't crossed by electric wires and that looked fairly level. One that had an access road for Lonnie, and wasn't ringed by a fence. Lonnie needed to get close enough, so that we wouldn't have to manually drag Ragtime Two across the field, or across barbed wire.

I explained to Margaret what we were looking for, and she studied the ground as we drifted, finally pointing to an area that was many, many acres clear, had an access road for Lonnie, and no obstructions that either of us could see.

"We're going down, Margaret. Call Lonnie and tell him where we're going to land." I gave her the route for him to follow.

"Tell him there's a white house to the left of a dirt road that'll lead him to the field."

"The owners won't mind?"

"I hope not, but Lonnie knows to stop at the house and ask permission for us to land. Usually it's after we've already landed, but we've never had anyone object. We try not to land on cows, or planted fields, but I don't see any around here, do you?"

"What if someone objected?"

"We'd just go someplace else."

Without heat, the air inside the envelope began to cool and slowly we began to drift lower. As we passed over the perimeter of the field, I began to release air. I wanted this to be a perfect landing. Margaret's only landing so far had been in the swamp, impaled on a tree limb, and hanging far above the ground.

This was going to be different.

We drifted lower, then Ragtime Two set us down upright, the envelope sagging, but still floating silently above us. It was the best landing I'd ever made. I was congratulating myself when I saw my truck bouncing towards us, followed by several pickups loaded with children. Probably the most exciting thing to happen to them.

We made friends immediately. Lonnie tied Ragtime Two to the bumper of my truck, and I inflated her just enough to give the children a quick lift, much to their squealing delight.

Under Lonnie's direction, the adults, women and men, helped him lay out the envelope, roll it into a ball and fit it into its canvas sack. Meanwhile I disassembled the basket supports, secured the instruments and lowered the Tommy Gate.

With everyone helping, we stored the basket and envelope in the back of the pickup, and I gave the grandfather, who owned the place, a printed thank-you for the use of his land as a hot-air balloon landing site. He was all grins as he showed the classy blue-and-gold certificate to his family.

"I loved it, Sarah," Margaret said as we closed our door behind us. "I have never experienced anything as exhilarating in my life!" She gave me a huge hug. "I'm hooked on ballooning, darling." She squeezed a little tighter. "After our experience the last time we flew together, I didn't think I'd ever say anything like that."

"That wasn't an ordinary flight. But then, nothing we do is ordinary." I snickered, thinking of last night. We were definitely not ordinary.

"We haven't had lunch. Take me to that little place for boudin?"

I managed to extract my arms from her absolutely crushing embrace. "Okay. Let's head out before some other hunger strikes."

"Does this other hunger supersede my craving for boudin?"

"You know better than to ask."

She pressed her mouth to mine, her hands inched under my shirt, claimed my breasts, and I heard, "I think I'll eat first, have boudin later."

"Much later," I said as I lowered her to the bed. "Much, much later."

A few of the publications of
THE NAIAD PRESS, INC.
P.O. Box 10543 • Tallahassee, Florida 32302
Phone (904) 539-5965
Toll-Free Order Number: 1-800-533-1973
Mail orders welcome. Please include 15% postage.

UP, UP AND AWAY by Catherine Ennis. 192 pp. Delightful
romance. ISBN 1-56280-065-5 $9.95

PERSONAL ADS by Robbi Sommers. 176 pp. Sizzling short
stories. ISBN 1-56280-059-0   9.95

FLASHPOINT by Katherine V. Forrest. 256 pp. Lesbian
blockbuster! ISBN 1-56280-043-4   22.95

CROSSWORDS by Penny Sumner. 256 pp. 2nd Victoria Cross
Mystery. ISBN 1-56280-064-7   9.95

SWEET CHERRY WINE by Carol Schmidt. 224 pp. A novel of
suspense. ISBN 1-56280-063-9   9.95

CERTAIN SMILES by Dorothy Tell. 160 pp. Erotic short stories.
ISBN 1-56280-066-3   9.95

EDITED OUT by Lisa Haddock. 224 pp. 1st Carmen Ramirez
Mystery. ISBN 1-56280-077-9   9.95

WEDNESDAY NIGHTS by Camarin Grae. 288 pp. Sexy
adventure. ISBN 1-56280-060-4   10.95

SMOKEY O by Celia Cohen. 176 pp. Relationships on the playing
field. ISBN 1-56280-057-4   9.95

KATHLEEN O'DONALD by Penny Hayes. 256 pp. Rose and
Kathleen find each other and employment in 1909 NYC.
ISBN 1-56280-070-1   9.95

STAYING HOME by Elisabeth Nonas. 256 pp. Molly and Alix
want a baby . . . or do they? ISBN 1-56280-076-0   10.95

TRUE LOVE by Jennifer Fulton. 240 pp. Six lesbians searching for
love in all the "right" places. ISBN 1-56280-035-3   9.95

GARDENIAS WHERE THERE ARE NONE by Molleen Zanger.
176 pp. Why is Melanie inextricably drawn to the old house?
ISBN 1-56280-056-6   9.95

MICHAELA by Sarah Aldridge. 256 pp. A "Sarah Aldridge"
romance. ISBN 1-56280-055-8   10.95

KEEPING SECRETS by Penny Mickelbury. 208 pp. A Gianna
Maglione Mystery. First in a series. ISBN 1-56280-052-3   9.95

THE ROMANTIC NAIAD edited by Katherine V. Forrest &
Barbara Grier. 336 pp. Love stories by Naiad Press authors.
                                    ISBN 1-56280-054-X   14.95

UNDER MY SKIN by Jaye Maiman. 336 pp. A Robin Miller
mystery. 3rd in a series.   ISBN 1-56280-049-3.   10.95

STAY TOONED by Rhonda Dicksion. 144 pp. Cartoons — 1st
collection since *Lesbian Survival Manual.*   ISBN 1-56280-045-0   9.95

CAR POOL by Karin Kallmaker. 272pp. Lesbians on wheels
and then some!   ISBN 1-56280-048-5   9.95

NOT TELLING MOTHER: STORIES FROM A LIFE by Diane
Salvatore. 176 pp. Her 3rd novel.   ISBN 1-56280-044-2   9.95

GOBLIN MARKET by Lauren Wright Douglas. 240pp. A Caitlin
Reece Mystery. 5th in a series.   ISBN 1-56280-047-7   9.95

LONG GOODBYES by Nikki Baker. 256 pp. A Virginia Kelly
mystery. 3rd in a series.   ISBN 1-56280-042-6   9.95

FRIENDS AND LOVERS by Jackie Calhoun. 224 pp. Mid-western
Lesbian lives and loves.   ISBN 1-56280-041-8   9.95

THE CAT CAME BACK by Hilary Mullins. 208 pp. Highly praised
Lesbian novel.   ISBN 1-56280-040-X   9.95

BEHIND CLOSED DOORS by Robbi Sommers. 192 pp. Hot, erotic
short stories.   ISBN 1-56280-039-6   9.95

CLAIRE OF THE MOON by Nicole Conn. 192 pp. See the movie —
read the book!   ISBN 1-56280-038-8   10.95

SILENT HEART by Claire McNab. 192 pp. Exotic Lesbian
romance.   ISBN 1-56280-036-1   9.95

HAPPY ENDINGS by Kate Brandt. 272 pp. Intimate conversations
with Lesbian authors.   ISBN 1-56280-050-7   10.95

THE SPY IN QUESTION by Amanda Kyle Williams. 256 pp. 4th
Madison McGuire.   ISBN 1-56280-037-X   9.95

SAVING GRACE by Jennifer Fulton. 240 pp. Adventure and
romantic entanglement.   ISBN 1-56280-051-5   9.95

THE YEAR SEVEN by Molleen Zanger. 208 pp. Women surviving
in a new world.   ISBN 1-56280-034-5   9.95

CURIOUS WINE by Katherine V. Forrest. 176 pp. Tenth
Anniversary Edition. The most popular contemporary Lesbian
love story.   ISBN 1-56280-053-1   10.95

CHAUTAUQUA by Catherine Ennis. 192 pp. Exciting, romantic
adventure.   ISBN 1-56280-032-9   9.95

A PROPER BURIAL by Pat Welch. 192 pp. A Helen Black
mystery. 3rd in a series.   ISBN 1-56280-033-7   9.95

SILVERLAKE HEAT: A Novel of Suspense by Carol Schmidt.
240 pp. Rhonda is as hot as Laney's dreams.   ISBN 1-56280-031-0   9.95

LOVE, ZENA BETH by Diane Salvatore. 224 pp. The most talked
about lesbian novel of the nineties!   ISBN 1-56280-030-2   9.95

A DOORYARD FULL OF FLOWERS by Isabel Miller. 160 pp.
Stories incl. 2 sequels to *Patience and Sarah*. ISBN 1-56280-029-9   9.95

MURDER BY TRADITION by Katherine V. Forrest. 288 pp. A
Kate Delafield Mystery. 4th in a series.   ISBN 1-56280-002-7   9.95

THE EROTIC NAIAD edited by Katherine V. Forrest & Barbara Grier.
224 pp. Love stories by Naiad Press authors.   ISBN 1-56280-026-4   12.95

DEAD CERTAIN by Claire McNab. 224 pp. A Carol Ashton
mystery. 5th in a series.   ISBN 1-56280-027-2   9.95

CRAZY FOR LOVING by Jaye Maiman. 320 pp. A Robin Miller
mystery. 2nd in a series.   ISBN 1-56280-025-6   9.95

STONEHURST by Barbara Johnson. 176 pp. Passionate regency
romance.   ISBN 1-56280-024-8   9.95

INTRODUCING AMANDA VALENTINE by Rose Beecham.
256 pp. An Amanda Valentine Mystery. First in a series.
                                             ISBN 1-56280-021-3   9.95

UNCERTAIN COMPANIONS by Robbi Sommers. 204 pp.
Steamy, erotic novel.   ISBN 1-56280-017-5   9.95

A TIGER'S HEART by Lauren W. Douglas. 240 pp. A Caitlin
Reece mystery. 4th in a series.   ISBN 1-56280-018-3   9.95

PAPERBACK ROMANCE by Karin Kallmaker. 256 pp. A
delicious romance.   ISBN 1-56280-019-1   9.95

MORTON RIVER VALLEY by Lee Lynch. 304 pp. Lee Lynch at
her best!   ISBN 1-56280-016-7   9.95

THE LAVENDER HOUSE MURDER by Nikki Baker. 224 pp. A
Virginia Kelly Mystery. 2nd in a series.   ISBN 1-56280-012-4   9.95

PASSION BAY by Jennifer Fulton. 224 pp. Passionate romance,
virgin beaches, tropical skies.   ISBN 1-56280-028-0   9.95

STICKS AND STONES by Jackie Calhoun. 208 pp. Contemporary
lesbian lives and loves.   ISBN 1-56280-020-5   9.95

DELIA IRONFOOT by Jeane Harris. 192 pp. Adventure for Delia
and Beth in the Utah mountains.   ISBN 1-56280-014-0   9.95

UNDER THE SOUTHERN CROSS by Claire McNab. 192 pp.
Romantic nights Down Under.   ISBN 1-56280-011-6   9.95

RIVERFINGER WOMEN by Elana Nachman/Dykewomon.
208 pp. Classic Lesbian/feminist novel.   ISBN 1-56280-013-2   8.95

A CERTAIN DISCONTENT by Cleve Boutell. 240 pp. A unique
coterie of women.   ISBN 1-56280-009-4   9.95

GRASSY FLATS by Penny Hayes. 256 pp. Lesbian romance in
the '30s.   ISBN 1-56280-010-8   9.95

A SINGULAR SPY by Amanda K. Williams. 192 pp. 3rd Madison
McGuire.   ISBN 1-56280-008-6   8.95

THE END OF APRIL by Penny Sumner. 240 pp. A Victoria Cross
Mystery. First in a series.   ISBN 1-56280-007-8   8.95

A FLIGHT OF ANGELS by Sarah Aldridge. 240 pp. Romance set at
the National Gallery of Art   ISBN 1-56280-001-9   9.95

HOUSTON TOWN by Deborah Powell. 208 pp. A Hollis Carpenter
mystery. Second in a series.   ISBN 1-56280-006-X   8.95

KISS AND TELL by Robbi Sommers. 192 pp. Scorching stories by
the author of *Pleasures*.   ISBN 1-56280-005-1   9.95

STILL WATERS by Pat Welch. 208 pp. A Helen Black mystery.
2nd in a series.   ISBN 0-941483-97-5   9.95

TO LOVE AGAIN by Evelyn Kennedy. 208 pp. Wildly
romantic love story.   ISBN 0-941483-85-1   9.95

IN THE GAME by Nikki Baker. 192 pp. A Virginia Kelly
mystery. First in a series.   ISBN 1-56280-004-3   9.95

AVALON by Mary Jane Jones. 256 pp. A Lesbian Arthurian
romance.   ISBN 0-941483-96-7   9.95

STRANDED by Camarin Grae. 320 pp. Entertaining, riveting
adventure.   ISBN 0-941483-99-1   9.95

THE DAUGHTERS OF ARTEMIS by Lauren Wright Douglas.
240 pp. A Caitlin Reece mystery. 3rd in a series.
                                      ISBN 0-941483-95-9   9.95

CLEARWATER by Catherine Ennis. 176 pp. Romantic secrets
of a small Louisiana town.   ISBN 0-941483-65-7   8.95

THE HALLELUJAH MURDERS by Dorothy Tell. 176 pp. A Poppy
Dillworth mystery. 2nd in a series.   ISBN 0-941483-88-6   8.95

ZETA BASE by Judith Alguire. 208 pp. Lesbian triangle
on a future Earth.   ISBN 0-941483-94-0   9.95

SECOND CHANCE by Jackie Calhoun. 256 pp. Contemporary
Lesbian lives and loves.   ISBN 0-941483-93-2   9.95

BENEDICTION by Diane Salvatore. 272 pp. Striking,
contemporary romantic novel.   ISBN 0-941483-90-8   9.95

CALLING RAIN by Karen Marie Christa Minns. 240 pp.
Spellbinding, erotic love story   ISBN 0-941483-87-8   9.95

BLACK IRIS by Jeane Harris. 192 pp. Caroline's hidden past . . .
                                      ISBN 0-941483-68-1   8.95

TOUCHWOOD by Karin Kallmaker. 240 pp. Loving, May/
December romance.   ISBN 0-941483-76-2   9.95

COP OUT by Claire McNab. 208 pp. A Carol Ashton mystery.
4th in a series.   ISBN 0-941483-84-3   9.95

LODESTAR by Phyllis Horn. 224 pp. Romantic, fast-moving
adventure.   ISBN 0-941483-83-5   8.95

THE BEVERLY MALIBU by Katherine V. Forrest. 288 pp. A
Kate Delafield Mystery. 3rd in a series.   ISBN 0-941483-48-7   9.95

THAT OLD STUDEBAKER by Lee Lynch. 272 pp. Andy's affair
with Regina and her attachment to her beloved car.
                 ISBN 0-941483-82-7   9.95

PASSION'S LEGACY by Lori Paige. 224 pp. Sarah is swept into
the arms of Augusta Pym in this delightful historical romance.
                 ISBN 0-941483-81-9   8.95

THE PROVIDENCE FILE by Amanda Kyle Williams. 256 pp.
Second Madison McGuire   ISBN 0-941483-92-4   8.95

I LEFT MY HEART by Jaye Maiman. 320 pp. A Robin Miller
Mystery. First in a series.   ISBN 0-941483-72-X   9.95

THE PRICE OF SALT by Patricia Highsmith (writing as Claire
Morgan). 288 pp. Classic lesbian novel, first issued in 1952 . . .
acknowledged by its author under her own, very famous, name.
                 ISBN 1-56280-003-5   9.95

SIDE BY SIDE by Isabel Miller. 256 pp. From beloved author of
Patience and Sarah.   ISBN 0-941483-77-0   9.95

STAYING POWER: LONG TERM LESBIAN COUPLES
by Susan E. Johnson. 352 pp. Joys of coupledom.
                 ISBN 0-941-483-75-4   12.95

SLICK by Camarin Grae. 304 pp. Exotic, erotic adventure.
                 ISBN 0-941483-74-6   9.95

NINTH LIFE by Lauren Wright Douglas. 256 pp. A Caitlin
Reece mystery. 2nd in a series.   ISBN 0-941483-50-9   8.95

PLAYERS by Robbi Sommers. 192 pp. Sizzling, erotic novel.
                 ISBN 0-941483-73-8   9.95

MURDER AT RED ROOK RANCH by Dorothy Tell. 224 pp.
A Poppy Dillworth mystery. 1st in a series.   ISBN 0-941483-80-0   8.95

LESBIAN SURVIVAL MANUAL by Rhonda Dicksion.
112 pp. Cartoons!   ISBN 0-941483-71-1   8.95

A ROOM FULL OF WOMEN by Elisabeth Nonas. 256 pp.
Contemporary Lesbian lives.   ISBN 0-941483-69-X   9.95

PRIORITIES by Lynda Lyons 288 pp. Science fiction with
a twist.   ISBN 0-941483-66-5   8.95

THEME FOR DIVERSE INSTRUMENTS by Jane Rule. 208
pp. Powerful romantic lesbian stories.   ISBN 0-941483-63-0   8.95

LESBIAN QUERIES by Hertz & Ertman. 112 pp. The questions
you were too embarrassed to ask.   ISBN 0-941483-67-3   8.95

CLUB 12 by Amanda Kyle Williams. 288 pp. Espionage thriller
featuring a lesbian agent!   ISBN 0-941483-64-9   8.95

DEATH DOWN UNDER by Claire McNab. 240 pp. A Carol
Ashton mystery. 3rd in a series.   ISBN 0-941483-39-8   9.95

MONTANA FEATHERS by Penny Hayes. 256 pp. Vivian and
Elizabeth find love in frontier Montana.   ISBN 0-941483-61-4   8.95

CHESAPEAKE PROJECT by Phyllis Horn. 304 pp. Jessie &
Meredith in perilous adventure.   ISBN 0-941483-58-4   8.95

LIFESTYLES by Jackie Calhoun. 224 pp. Contemporary Lesbian
lives and loves.   ISBN 0-941483-57-6   9.95

VIRAGO by Karen Marie Christa Minns. 208 pp. Darsen has
chosen Ginny.   ISBN 0-941483-56-8   8.95

WILDERNESS TREK by Dorothy Tell. 192 pp. Six women on
vacation learning "new" skills.   ISBN 0-941483-60-6   8.95

MURDER BY THE BOOK by Pat Welch. 256 pp. A Helen
Black Mystery. First in a series.   ISBN 0-941483-59-2   9.95

LESBIANS IN GERMANY by Lillian Faderman & B. Eriksson.
128 pp. Fiction, poetry, essays.   ISBN 0-941483-62-2   8.95

THERE'S SOMETHING I'VE BEEN MEANING TO TELL
YOU Ed. by Loralee MacPike. 288 pp. Gay men and lesbians
coming out to their children.   ISBN 0-941483-44-4   9.95

LIFTING BELLY by Gertrude Stein. Ed. by Rebecca Mark. 104
pp. Erotic poetry.   ISBN 0-941483-51-7   8.95

ROSE PENSKI by Roz Perry. 192 pp. Adult lovers in a long-term
relationship.   ISBN 0-941483-37-1   8.95

AFTER THE FIRE by Jane Rule. 256 pp. Warm, human novel
by this incomparable author.   ISBN 0-941483-45-2   8.95

SUE SLATE, PRIVATE EYE by Lee Lynch. 176 pp. The gay
folk of Peacock Alley are *all cats.*   ISBN 0-941483-52-5   8.95

CHRIS by Randy Salem. 224 pp. Golden oldie. Handsome Chris
and her adventures.   ISBN 0-941483-42-8   8.95

THREE WOMEN by March Hastings. 232 pp. Golden oldie. A
triangle among wealthy sophisticates.   ISBN 0-941483-43-6   8.95

RICE AND BEANS by Valeria Taylor. 232 pp. Love and
romance on poverty row.   ISBN 0-941483-41-X   8.95

PLEASURES by Robbi Sommers. 204 pp. Unprecedented
eroticism.   ISBN 0-941483-49-5   8.95

EDGEWISE by Camarin Grae. 372 pp. Spellbinding
adventure.   ISBN 0-941483-19-3   9.95

FATAL REUNION by Claire McNab. 224 pp. A Carol Ashton
mystery. 2nd in a series.   ISBN 0-941483-40-1   8.95

KEEP TO ME STRANGER by Sarah Aldridge. 372 pp. Romance
set in a department store dynasty.   ISBN 0-941483-38-X   9.95

IN THE BLOOD by Lauren Wright Douglas. 252 pp. Lesbian
science fiction adventure fantasy   ISBN 0-941483-22-3   8.95

THE BEE'S KISS by Shirley Verel. 216 pp. Delicate, delicious
romance.   ISBN 0-941483-36-3   8.95

RAGING MOTHER MOUNTAIN by Pat Emmerson. 264 pp.
Furosa Firechild's adventures in Wonderland.   ISBN 0-941483-35-5   8.95

IN EVERY PORT by Karin Kallmaker. 228 pp. Jessica's sexy,
adventuresome travels.   ISBN 0-941483-37-7   9.95

OF LOVE AND GLORY by Evelyn Kennedy. 192 pp. Exciting
WWII romance.   ISBN 0-941483-32-0   8.95

CLICKING STONES by Nancy Tyler Glenn. 288 pp. Love
transcending time.   ISBN 0-941483-31-2   9.95

SURVIVING SISTERS by Gail Pass. 252 pp. Powerful love
story.   ISBN 0-941483-16-9   8.95

SOUTH OF THE LINE by Catherine Ennis. 216 pp. Civil War
adventure.   ISBN 0-941483-29-0   8.95

WOMAN PLUS WOMAN by Dolores Klaich. 300 pp. Supurb
Lesbian overview.   ISBN 0-941483-28-2   9.95

THE FINER GRAIN by Denise Ohio. 216 pp. Brilliant young
college lesbian novel.   ISBN 0-941483-11-8   8.95

HIGH CONTRAST by Jessie Lattimore. 264 pp. Women of the
Crystal Palace.   ISBN 0-941483-17-7   8.95

OCTOBER OBSESSION by Meredith More. Josie's rich, secret
Lesbian life.   ISBN 0-941483-18-5   8.95

BEFORE STONEWALL: THE MAKING OF A GAY AND
LESBIAN COMMUNITY by Andrea Weiss & Greta Schiller.
96 pp., 25 illus.   ISBN 0-941483-20-7   7.95

WE WALK THE BACK OF THE TIGER by Patricia A. Murphy.
192 pp. Romantic Lesbian novel/beginning women's movement.
                                           ISBN 0-941483-13-4   8.95

SUNDAY'S CHILD by Joyce Bright. 216 pp. Lesbian athletics, at
last the novel about sports.   ISBN 0-941483-12-6   8.95

OSTEN'S BAY by Zenobia N. Vole. 204 pp. Sizzling adventure
romance set on Bonaire.   ISBN 0-941483-15-0   8.95

LESSONS IN MURDER by Claire McNab. 216 pp. A Carol
Ashton mystery. First in a series.   ISBN 0-941483-14-2   9.95

YELLOWTHROAT by Penny Hayes. 240 pp. Margarita, bandit,
kidnaps Julia.   ISBN 0-941483-10-X   8.95

SAPPHISTRY: THE BOOK OF LESBIAN SEXUALITY by
Pat Califia. 3d edition, revised. 208 pp.   ISBN 0-941483-24-X   10.95

CHERISHED LOVE by Evelyn Kennedy. 192 pp. Erotic
Lesbian love story.   ISBN 0-941483-08-8   9.95

LAST SEPTEMBER by Helen R. Hull. 208 pp. Six stories & a
glorious novella.   ISBN 0-941483-09-6   8.95

THE SECRET IN THE BIRD by Camarin Grae. 312 pp. Striking,
psychological suspense novel.   ISBN 0-941483-05-3   8.95

TO THE LIGHTNING by Catherine Ennis. 208 pp. Romantic
Lesbian 'Robinson Crusoe' adventure.   ISBN 0-941483-06-1   8.95

THE OTHER SIDE OF VENUS by Shirley Verel. 224 pp.
Luminous, romantic love story.   ISBN 0-941483-07-X   8.95

DREAMS AND SWORDS by Katherine V. Forrest. 192 pp.
Romantic, erotic, imaginative stories.   ISBN 0-941483-03-7   8.95

MEMORY BOARD by Jane Rule. 336 pp. Memorable novel
about an aging Lesbian couple.   ISBN 0-941483-02-9   9.95

THE ALWAYS ANONYMOUS BEAST by Lauren Wright
Douglas. 224 pp. A Caitlin Reece mystery. First in a series.
                                              ISBN 0-941483-04-5   8.95

DUSTY'S QUEEN OF HEARTS DINER by Lee Lynch. 240 pp.
Romantic blue-collar novel.   ISBN 0-941483-01-0   8.95

PARENTS MATTER by Ann Muller. 240 pp. Parents'
relationships with Lesbian daughters and gay sons.
                                              ISBN 0-930044-91-6   9.95

MAGDALENA by Sarah Aldridge. 352 pp. Epic Lesbian novel
set on three continents.   ISBN 0-930044-99-1   8.95

THE BLACK AND WHITE OF IT by Ann Allen Shockley.
144 pp. Short stories.   ISBN 0-930044-96-7   7.95

SAY JESUS AND COME TO ME by Ann Allen Shockley. 288
pp. Contemporary romance.   ISBN 0-930044-98-3   8.95

LOVING HER by Ann Allen Shockley. 192 pp. Romantic love
story.   ISBN 0-930044-97-5   7.95

MURDER AT THE NIGHTWOOD BAR by Katherine V.
Forrest. 240 pp. A Kate Delafield mystery. Second in a series.
                                              ISBN 0-930044-92-4   10.95

ZOE'S BOOK by Gail Pass. 224 pp. Passionate, obsessive love
story.   ISBN 0-930044-95-9   7.95

WINGED DANCER by Camarin Grae. 228 pp. Erotic Lesbian
adventure story.   ISBN 0-930044-88-6   8.95

PAZ by Camarin Grae. 336 pp. Romantic Lesbian adventurer
with the power to change the world.   ISBN 0-930044-89-4   8.95

SOUL SNATCHER by Camarin Grae. 224 pp. A puzzle, an
adventure, a mystery — Lesbian romance.   ISBN 0-930044-90-8   8.95

THE LOVE OF GOOD WOMEN by Isabel Miller. 224 pp.
Long-awaited new novel by the author of the beloved *Patience
and Sarah.*   ISBN 0-930044-81-9   8.95

THE HOUSE AT PELHAM FALLS by Brenda Weathers. 240
pp. Suspenseful Lesbian ghost story.   ISBN 0-930044-79-7   7.95

HOME IN YOUR HANDS by Lee Lynch. 240 pp. More stories
from the author of *Old Dyke Tales.*   ISBN 0-930044-80-0   7.95

SURPLUS by Sylvia Stevenson. 342 pp. A classic early Lesbian
novel.   ISBN 0-930044-78-9   7.95

PEMBROKE PARK by Michelle Martin. 256 pp. Derring-do
and daring romance in Regency England.   ISBN 0-930044-77-0   7.95

THE LONG TRAIL by Penny Hayes. 248 pp. Vivid adventures
of two women in love in the old west.   ISBN 0-930044-76-2   8.95

AN EMERGENCE OF GREEN by Katherine V. Forrest. 288
pp. Powerful novel of sexual discovery.   ISBN 0-930044-69-X   9.95

THE LESBIAN PERIODICALS INDEX edited by Claire
Potter. 432 pp. Author & subject index.   ISBN 0-930044-74-6   12.95

DESERT OF THE HEART by Jane Rule. 224 pp. A classic;
basis for the movie *Desert Hearts.*   ISBN 0-930044-73-8   9.95

FOR KEEPS by Elisabeth Nonas. 144 pp. Contemporary novel
about losing and finding love.   ISBN 0-930044-71-1   7.95

TORCHLIGHT TO VALHALLA by Gale Wilhelm. 128 pp.
Classic novel by a great Lesbian writer.   ISBN 0-930044-68-1   7.95

LESBIAN NUNS: BREAKING SILENCE edited by Rosemary
Curb and Nancy Manahan. 432 pp. Unprecedented autobiographies
of religious life.   ISBN 0-930044-62-2   9.95

THE SWASHBUCKLER by Lee Lynch. 288 pp. Colorful novel
set in Greenwich Village in the sixties.   ISBN 0-930044-66-5   8.95

MISFORTUNE'S FRIEND by Sarah Aldridge. 320 pp. Histori-
cal Lesbian novel set on two continents.   ISBN 0-930044-67-3   7.95

SEX VARIANT WOMEN IN LITERATURE by Jeannette
Howard Foster. 448 pp. Literary history.   ISBN 0-930044-65-7   8.95

These are just a few of the many Naiad Press titles — we are the oldest and
largest lesbian/feminist publishing company in the world. Please request a
complete catalog. We offer personal service; we encourage and welcome direct
mail orders from individuals who have limited access to bookstores carrying
our publications.